THE ORGANIZER

Lili,
Enjoy the book

[signature]

THE ORGANIZER

Peter Fogu Sr. and Thomas Fogu Sr.

iUniverse, Inc.
New York Lincoln Shanghai

The Organizer

iUniverse books may be ordered through booksellers or by contacting:

iUniverse
2021 Pine Lake Road, Suite 100
Lincoln, NE 68512
www.iuniverse.com
1-800-Authors (1-800-288-4677)

ISBN-13: 978-0-595-38142-5 (pbk)
ISBN-13: 978-0-595-82633-9 (cloth)
ISBN-13: 978-0-595-82510-3 (ebk)
ISBN-10: 0-595-38142-1 (pbk)
ISBN-10: 0-595-82633-4 (cloth)
ISBN-10: 0-595-82510-9 (ebk)

Printed in the United States of America

Dedicated to Peter Fogu Sr.
1925–1990

To my Dad for without
him this book would
have not been written.
We miss you very much.

CONTENTS

▼

CHAPTER 1

▼

MARY

Chapter One

I was thinking of Mary. The year was 1945, and like a trapped fly, felt help-less. The war had not been kind to me—I was hardened and scarred inter-nally. But if ever God could send an angel, he certainly sent one to me.

She was breathtaking to look at, and I was the lucky guy she chose. Slowly, a serene way of life returned and those war years of hell slipped away when I met her—my Mary—the wonderful, the beautiful Mary. And I mar-ried her.

Even now, the tears fill my eyes as I remember the kindness in her heart, her soft, auburn hair, the color of the trees' leaves during autumn. The end-less hours she spent sitting on our porch, particularly in the summer. Never mind if it was too hot and she was sweating, she always kept an eye out to make sure our sons and the neighbors' children were safe when they played outside. She was like that...sweet and caring, whether she knew you or not. She was the type who would go out of her way to save a helpless stray puppy from the street and then wouldn't complain when it soiled the carpet. "Just a puppy, Tom," she would say, "how can you blame a baby?" Her kind-ness...it could fill at least twenty oceans.

At Christmas time, she did the house up with hundreds of those little lights you could buy at Woolworth's. There were ribbons and sparkling dec-orations hanging from all the windows and porch, with the smell of holiday treats in the air. I would arrive home and smell homemade chocolates, freshly baked gingerbread cookies in the shapes of stars and Christmas trees, and sweet vanilla iced angel food cake along with mince and apple pies. Bak-ing desserts was Mary's specialty. Just before Christmas, we would all go and pick out a tree, and Mary would take the boys to visit Santa Claus at the local department store. She was a special mother. I remember her giggling that night, the first year when she hid behind the huge Santa throne and lis-tened to what the boys asked Santa for. "I wrote them all down, Tom" she whispered, as if the sleeping children upstairs could hear her. Just that look of sheer joy on her face and I would melt, giving her all the money she wanted to buy the gifts. My boys and I sure were lucky to have received this special angel from God.

Our marriage was blissful and we were blessed with three beautiful chil-dren. I had a prospering business, and for many years our lives were filled with love. Even now, I still don't understand why God can be so benevolent and give you such golden joy, and then—with no warning or justification—

take it away. I don't suppose I'll ever understand why God does the things he does—but then again—maybe we're not meant too.

Suddenly, everything shattered. Practically overnight, my dearest possession, my Mary, my beloved wife, was taken from me. I look back now and remember, so clearly, all the signs—the little things—that at the time seemed so meaningless. I should have forced her to go to the doctor, but she always refused. She won every argument. "Oh, it's just a little acid stomach, Tom" she would say. "I'm just a little bloated, Tom…have to watch the salt." But it wasn't any of that, was it Mary?

I should have done more, especially when I knew she had been vomiting regularly for a few weeks. But she always had an answer, and I was much more content to just believe her explanations than to admit that something might be wrong. "Oh, I just ate the wrong thing," or "I just have a sensitive stomach," or "have to watch what I eat, that's all, Tom." Hell, what did I know? Maybe she was just pregnant again.

If she knew anything more serious than an upset stomach was happening to her, she never let on. But that's exactly who she was—never wanting to burden anyone with anything painful. How could God have kept such a terrible secret from me? It was cancer. Then, on Good Friday, I came home to find the ambulance at my door, just two short days later, my Mary was dead in my arms at the age of thirty-one. And just like that, on Easter Sunday, our three boys and I were left alone.

For more than six months I drank myself into oblivion. Life lost it's meaning for me as I tried to drown my sorrow with each gulp of Jack Daniels. I couldn't even look at our boys anymore. All I could see in their faces was my beautiful beloved Mary, lost forever. I couldn't take care of them. I was spending more time with the bottle than my store, and my business was failing. Where was the money going to come from to raise them? I would have to sell everything.

I was now living in a small town that was suddenly dry and cold to me. Old customers just shook their heads now as they looked at the town's drunk—a bottle a day, down-on-his-luck loser. They gossiped about me. They sometimes talked just loud enough for me to hear them say that I was no good. Here I was throwing it all away, instead of being the man of the house, stoically holding my family together.

After a while, no one showed me any sympathy. Did no one out there know what it was like to lose, over and over again, as if you were never supposed to have a chance? Did no one out there know what it meant to be crushed—completely crushed—externally and internally?

My deceased wife's mother took the boys in, but she really was too old. Soon it was Christmas, but not a good one. It was our first without Mary. Grandma tried to bring in the holiday spirit, for the boys' sake, but the lights and tree, and the baked goodies all seemed empty. I started December with my bottle of Jack in hand, and then realized my store was closed and up for sale. I had no money to give Grandma for her extra expenses all these months, and I almost forgot to show up on Christmas. It was the first Christmas that no one bought any of the presents my sons asked Santa for.

I stayed drunk that day. I knew our youngest didn't notice much. He still played with the pitiful present I brought him. I told him his mother was still away visiting a sick aunt, but the others knew. They hated me. Grandma and I had an argument late at night, and it was decided. I had to place them in a Catholic home for wayward boys. Would my sons ever forgive me? I doubt it. At least they would have a roof over their head and schooling. And, my love for them? Even that was being questioned. My heart was broken. I don't think there was a piece of it left, not even for them.

All my life it seemed, that no sooner did a path open for me, then God took it away. First it was the war, then Mary's death, a failing business, then finally, losing my boys. I was headed towards disaster. This was the roughest depression I had ever known. I like to think that if I had only known, before those first steps into the quicksand, how destructive my path would become that I would have taken a different direction. However, my soothsayer did not exist, and I stepped blindly.

Somehow, I tried to get on and find some small spark of life buried deep inside me. I often looked at her crumpled picture that I kept in my pocket. She would have wanted me to go on. I know that. I guess I was not the man she had told me I was. I don't know why, but I guess I just gave up for a while.

I moved away with not much more than the clothes on my back, barely affording a room at a boarding house. I had to sell everything. I thought I would look for work that would not remind me of everything I had lost. When that didn't work out (everything reminded me of her) I turned to thievery. It was easy to creep around at night at the boarding house and go through people's pockets and bundles, but I knew I was on borrowed time. If I got caught, it was the slammer for a home. One day, I downed my usual shot of Jack, washed up to look a little presentable, and took my pennies for a cheap breakfast. There was a sign posted at the diner. A local, non-union shop was hiring. At least it was something I could do as I had picked up the trade during the war. I only had to stay away from the booze a little.

I was hired. It was easy...a battered, World War II vet...just lost his childhood sweetheart and wife of ten years with three boys to raise. I painted quite a picture for them...I always had that gift of gab. I lied a little...my sons were staying with a relative until I could get going again. They questioned me as to whether I cared if it was a non-union shop. I had very little opinion on that, which seemed to seal the job for me. Like most people, it didn't matter much to me. But this too would change.

Well it was a start, a job at least. Nobody knew me here and I had a clean slate. Little did I know, that this job would lead me to a smokier world filled with adventure, money, love again, and a new kind of hell—worse than the one I was already living.

That day, the sun was shining brighter inside me than it had in a while when I walked into the shop. Work was good for me. It was a special healer that pushed away my loneliness and despair. I felt useful again and punched my time card as usual. Just as I started towards the machinery, I heard my name.

"Tom!"

It was the foreman. I turned around and answered back with a smile.

"Yeah, Bill? How are you?"

"Fine, fine. Could you come into the back of the shop? I'm having a little meeting with the men...you need to hear this too."

We walked toward the rear of the shop and I noticed the entire crew was there, including the night shift. Bill was passing cards out to everyone. I looked at mine and saw it had something to do with a union. Before I could read any further, I was interrupted by Bill's explanation.

"Men, we've decided to bring a union to this shop and I want you all to join. Now a union is a good thing to have. There are lots of benefits, but I'm not here to tell you how unions can help you. I'll let them do that." Bill shifted his weight nervously and continued. "The union that we selected seems to be the best one for us. Those cards that you have in your hands will let them represent us. I want all these cards returned to me when the shifts are over, and I expect them all to be signed. That's right, I said I wann'em signed. That means each and every one of you. Well, that's all I have to say, so get back to work..."

My internal response was a mixture of fear and anger. I returned to the shop floor dizzy almost, as all kinds of unanswered questions began to flood my brain. What the hell was this all about? Was my boss telling me I had to sign this card even if I didn't want to? What would happen if I didn't? Would I lose my job? What, more bad times, as if I didn't have enough of that? I didn't know much about unions. I didn't care much about them but why this union in particular? And why would a foreman tell us we had to sign these cards? Who would benefit—him or me?

A funny feeling started to build in the pit of my stomach. With each passing thought it became worse. In fact, the entire business sounded a little bit too suspicious and one-sided. It smelled bad, very bad. This was the first hint that maybe my life was starting to turn around—I actually cared about something other than losing Mary.

During lunch, small groups started to gather around the shop. The chief topic of conversation was about signing the cards. Some rebelled like I had about being told that we had to join, others were indifferent. Still, others wanted to join. Yet, no one could see my growing apprehension. The ones who readily consented to sign the cards were the foremen and the ones with high positions and pay. It wasn't the workers. The men who signed didn't need the union benefits.

Keep out of this Tom, I kept repeating to myself. Don't get involved. But after the lunch bell had rung and everyone returned to work, the atmosphere had changed. Workers were signing their cards but not willingly. Friction and fear were embedded in them...fear of losing their jobs, their homes, their families, if they didn't join.

When I heard the quitting bell, I was relieved and over anxious to leave in order to get out of signing the card. It could wait until tomorrow, I told myself. The enthusiasm I had for my job began to wane. The sun was still shining as I walked into the street and the air was crisp and enlivening, but this did nothing to lift my feelings. I was dejected and I was scared.

A hand suddenly touched my shoulder. I quickly turned and encountered a well dressed, small built man. His handsome features and warm, wide smile were beguiling. I liked him immediately.

"Hello. My name is Vincent Cerboto, got a minute?"

"Yeah, sure. What?"

I thought he was lost, maybe, and needed directions.

"I'd appreciate it, if you'd listen to what I have to say," he continued.

He wrapped his arm around my shoulder and walked with me in the direction of my car.

"There's going to be a big controversy. I wanted to warn you. In your shop there's going to be two different unions battling each other. You already have come in contact with one and I represent the other. All I ask is that you listen to our side of the story."

"Listen?…I don't know Pal, it's been a long day."

"But we're the best union! This will only take a few minutes…"

"All right, I'll listen, but don't you represent the whole industry?"

"No, we represent only our own union. And we're the best!"

"I thought that all the unions worked together."

"Like I said, you already came in contact with one union. Why not listen about ours? Hear us out and give yourself a chance to make the right decision. We're having a meeting tonight. Are you free? It's at our hall on Fifty-Seventh Street and I'd appreciate it, if you could be there."

He handed me a small flyer announcing the meeting. I knew I was getting into something over my head, but the spark of excitement, even adventure in my gut told me to go. Do it!

"Okay. I'll try to make it."

"It's for YOU! This is all for YOU! You go to this meeting. You won't regret it. You'll see…just hear us out. I'll see you later. OKAY?"

He shook my hand strongly with both his hands clasping mine as his wide, enticing smile engaged my gaze. I watched as he spun around and practically broke into a jig going up to another worker leaving the shop.

The sun was slipping away and I wondered if this was an omen. A sky filled with a medley of colors as the sun set with a slim sliver of a moon poking through…all the day's headaches, tossing's and turnings about unions and card signing's, and now this man…he slipped away into the distance after sneaking up on me out of the blue with his warm, warm handshake still embedded in my palm. Yes, I would go. Why not take the chance? Maybe no sooner did God take away the day's light, did he open up another pathway.

CHAPTER 2

▼

THE BIG MAN

Chapter Two

I and a few others entered the large union hall. It could easily sit a hundred people and was filled practically to capacity. I was surprised to see so many of my fellow workers sitting there, their attention focused on two men up-front. One was perched on top of a large office desk with his legs dangling over the side. He was a big, burly man about six feet five, three hundred and twenty pounds, fifty-two or three with jet black hair that was greased up and slicked back. He was dressed immaculately in a white shirt, tailored suit and a big Cuban cigar. We had interrupted his speech and he paused. The room went silent as I tried to find a seat.

"For the benefit of all newcomers, my name is John Gervonte, and I represent the best, most powerful union in this town! I want the chance to represent your shop. You must know by now that another union is trying to push itself on you. That would be alright if it were the right union for you, but it isn't! We are the BEST! Your boss invited this other union into your shop. And when a boss does that, you can bet that the only one to gain is your boss himself! Whattaya think of that? You want a union for your boss' benefit, not yours? No way! Think of what you'll receive with us instead. If you don't already know, a boss sponsored union only gives you what your boss approves of. Is that what you want? Wouldn't you want a union working strictly for you?...Just you alone?"

The hall was quiet, as quiet as when I first walked in interrupting his speech. The big man shifted his body slowly swinging his feet until they touched the floor. Then he raised himself to his full height and walked over to the front row of seats and stood there, towering above us, surveying the crowd. The audience was concentrating on every word.

"Now about this union that's trying to control your lives, and mind you, has the full consent of your boss. Any union that would openly consort with your boss isn't worth a dime. They're not working for your interests. Does your boss work for you? No!...We should consider them crooks and outlaws."

"Yes, I repeat, crooks! They're out to steal your money...the money you worked so hard to earn. Your employer doesn't seem to think you have any brains to realize just how they're operating, but I think different. In fact, I know different!" Then silence. Now he shouted even louder.

"Your boss is lying to you. Are you gonna allow your employer and his union to get together and cheat you out of what is rightfully yours? Say NO! Are you gonna let 'em steal from you? I said, say NO!"

A few "noes", a few "what's this about?" and "the boss lied to us?" rippled through the hall as slow whispers. My friends and co-workers leaned forward…the seats, themselves, seemed to move closer to this big man.

"Don't let 'em in! You need your own union—a union like ours who will work for YOU, the workers, not your employer. And we'll give you our damn'est to get you every benefit you deserve, and even more!"

The big man paused and starting picking up several packs of cards from the table. "Cards will be passed out to you and I would like everyone to sign them. Your John Hancock, right here, is your personal invitation to allow us to represent your shop. It looks like a good turn-out tonight—it won't be long before you control your shop. Your union should work for YOU!"

A spark ignited inside of me as I felt the sharp tingle of excitement rise. I could no longer remain quiet and rose to my feet, hesitantly, but determined to speak.

"Sir? Can I ask you something? Is that okay, here?"

The Big Man's eyes caught mine as everyone in the hall turned in their seats to watch me.

"Yes?"

"You say the majority of workers are here and you're positive that when we sign these cards you will control the shop."

"No, YOU will—all of YOU will control the shop!" He answered quickly.

"But, what will happen if EVERYONE doesn't join? What will happen when our boss finds out we've gone behind his back? He could retaliate."

The big man swung his arms as if to embrace the audience.

"If we have to, we'll strike! But you are the ones who will decide that!"

"But, if we strike," I continued, "if we have to strike and the rest of the shop just passes the picket line, what then? We have friends who aren't here and if they think the boss's union is better for us, I don't see why friends should fight each other over a difference of opinion."

"This is not just a difference of opinion. You're gonna lose with your boss's choice of unions. And, if we're forced to strike," he said calmly, "and a picket line is necessary then that will be my problem, not yours. For the first couple of days we'll run the picket line for you. No one in this room will be forced to get on the line. We have our own workers who will take care of any interference, and if anyone wants to get tough, well, we can take care of that too! We wrote the book on that subject!"

I interrupted, couldn't stop myself. Words started pouring out of me as I began to feel I represented the whole audience.

"In other words," I said, "this is a fight between two unions to see who gets all the spoils?"

We debated, the Big Man, this union leader, and me. The union hall took on the appearance of a tennis court with the audience's faces automatically bouncing from one speaker to the other.

No one else had the guts to even talk. I was dissatisfied with the way everything was being handled and everyone seemed to know it. I wanted answers and I was determined to get them!

"And another thing. Just what is your union offering us? You've been telling us that we need a union in our shop. Our boss is giving us no choice in this matter. Now, two unions are fighting for our shop? So, what does your union have that the other union can't match?"

The Big Man whispered something to the other man sitting up front. He rose and quietly left the room, and the Big Man continued.

"When the time comes, we'll make up a list of all the items that will improve your working conditions. We'll increase your wages. We'll improve your working conditions, give you more time off for sickness, more vacation days, the works. Then we'll draw up a contract, and after you have approved it, of course, we will present it to your employer. If he signs the contract, we have no problems."

My train of thought remained the same. I still couldn't see much difference between the two unions. Wouldn't they both promise the world to everyone? With noticeable annoyance in my voice, I confronted the Big Man once again.

"But what exactly are the advantages of joining your union over the other?"

The audience began murmuring.

"We'll give you hospitalization," he said.

"So can they," I replied.

"We'll try to get you seven holidays."

"We get six right now, they're offering eight."

"This union will get you less working hours with more pay."

"Oh come on now. We get all the overtime we can handle. There isn't a single person in this room who doesn't take home good pay. Of course, we'd like a little more, but what the other union is offering is similar, or in some cases, better benefits than yours. So once, again, why should we choose you?"

"We could offer you the moon just as they are, but can they get it for you? What good are empty promises? We can make good on what we say! We are organized! We know this business! We already have a success record with other shops. We are the BEST and we should represent you. At least we're gonna try like hell to win your approval, one hundred percent! And know this…to date, we have never approached your employer. We only work for you, the workers, and we have been solely representing only shops in your line of work. We don't branch into different fields. We've investigated down to the most insignificant detail, every phase of this type of work, and we've been doing this for years. The other union can't even touch us when it comes to the experience we have in this line of work. We'll find out what you want, and we'll tell you what you need. When we deal with your employer, we demand for you! When we draw up a contract, we go beyond expectations to win your boss's signature. Now isn't it better to have a union who thoroughly knows your line of work? Won't we be better qualified to represent you than your boss' union who is just so green. His union will just use you to make an entrance into this field and control you."

"Oh," I started to say, but was interrupted. The door opened and the man who had left returned with some other men carrying packages, steaming pots of freshly, brewed coffee, sandwiches, and coffee cake. Cigarettes, cigars and pamphlets were passed out throughout the audience. The audience welcomed the interruption. It helped clear the friction in the air.

"Let's take a break" the Big Man said. "Let's all have some coffee and cake." He smiled at everyone and began shaking hands in front of the hall, but he never stopped eyeing me. Slowly, he began to make his way to where I was standing.

It was then I knew I was bucking a pro. I had started a confrontation and he knew how to cut it short. Our debate had been temporarily halted as everyone started towards the refreshments.

Suddenly a hand was on my shoulder. I turned and saw it was Vincent, the fellow I encountered just a few hours ago when I left the shop.

"Can I see you for a moment Tom? I have something you might be interested in. Here, let's talk in the office."

He motioned with his head what direction to take, to my right. We walked down a corridor. Several groups of people chatting in the foyer area, gave way to an emptier, longer hallway, lined with locked doors and silence. Then we arrived at this one particular door…at the very end.

Vincent opened the door for me and we walked in. The Big Man and two other men were sitting at the desk already.

"Sit down, Tom," Vincent said.

Trouble, I said to myself. This did not feel like a friendly meeting. It felt like an ambush.

"This is John Gervonte, who you just spoke with in the hall."

I shook his hand firmly, "Pleased to meet you. Sorry if I caused a ruckus in there. I didn't mean anything disrespectful."

"No offence taken. What's your name?" John asked.

"Thomas Furcco."

The Big Man took control continuing with the introductions.

"You already met, Vincent, and you know me. This here, is John Funoto and this is Mike Ternille."

Before I could acknowledge the introductions, Mike asked, "What the fuck have you got against unions?"

"Nothing," I said. "I just don't want to get involved in the middle of a union fight. The people out there don't know what's going on, but I do. It seems to me that a fight between unions means we people don't mean a thing to either union. Each union is fighting to be in control and they'll use us to do their work. I'm sorry I had to say that, no offense."

"That's okay, Tom," Vincent said, while the Big Man started to smile at me.

"What do you do in your shop, Tom?" Gervonte asked.

"I'm a mechanic."

"Been in the service?"

"Yeah, five years, overseas."

"So you saw some action?"

"Some." The questions were getting personal, and my answers shorter. I didn't like the direction this conversation was taking.

"How about your schooling, Tom?"

"High school diploma, year of college. Better than most."

"Any family?"

"My wife recently passed. "I started to look anxiously towards the doorway. Why were they asking me these personal questions? What was up here exactly or should I just nip this in the bud and leave?

"Any Children?"

"No." I lied

"How long have you been in this shop, Tom? You haven't been in it for long then, have you?"

I stood up, somewhat irritated and angry. What the hell did all this talk have to do with unions? If you have something to say, say it, and get it over with.

"No, I haven't been at the shop for long. What the hell difference does that make?"

The Big Man looked at me from across his desk and without taking his eyes off of me, he spoke to everyone else.

"Mike, can you and John leave?...Vincent, you stay...Tom, we have something to talk to you about...alone."

"Nice meeting you, Tom."

"Yeah, you too."

The two men rose from their chairs and left. John's glance was still on me as I sat back down in my chair trying to relax.

"Can you get on the night shift?" he asked, somewhat cunningly.

That was a question out of the blue. I suppose I could if I wanted too. The night shift was not a popular one and they did need a man on the late shift.

"Why? What does this have to do with unions?"

"It has to be the graveyard shift, twelve to eight." He hadn't answered my question.

"But why that shift and why me? What'd we talking about exactly?"

"Tom, I like you. You're honest. We're looking for enterprising men— someone who will stand up for what he believes in and others will listen too—and to me, you seem to fit the bill. You have something on the ball...brains, and I don't wanna see you waste your life in a small shop. I'm a pretty good judge of people, and after that session in the hall, I know a lot about you already. You have stamina, perseverance, and most of all, you have balls! And that's something you need plenty of when you join our union."

"Join us, Tom. Join our union," Vincent said. "We want you to work for us."

That took me by surprise. Here I was fighting them openly, verbally, and now they were offering me a job? The words, "join our union...join us Tom" spun through my brain.

"About the twelve to eight shift, that's perfect for what I have in mind. You will come in contact with the day shift when you leave, and the night shift when you start. This also eliminates the foremen because without them, you'll be able to talk more freely with other workers."

"Talk to them? About what?"

"I feel you have what it takes to persuade the men to join our side. And when you do, we'll gain control. Your department runs the whole place. If your machines are closed down, nothing can operate. If you don't make any material, they'll have none to ship. It's that simple. Also, after we throw up a picket line, that graveyard shift will enable you to come and go as you please. Whattaya you say, Tom?"

"Look, no offense, but I don't even know if I want to join your union. And if I did accept your offer, what do I get? A promise of a job?"

"How much are you making, Tom?"

"Seventy-five a week."

"I'll give you another seventy-five a week for as long as the strike lasts. If you get the men to walk out, another bonus of three hundred and fifty will be waiting for you. Now how does that sound to you?"

I sat there, unable to reply at first. Earning that much money for such little work. I had never been able to make a fast buck—all my previous earnings had come through hard work. Now here was this opportunity to make some money, maybe get my family back, all I had to do was get my co-workers to join this union.

"And, all I have to do is talk to the other workers and convince 'em to support your walk out? I've never done anything like this before in my life."

"Yeah, Tom, that's all. You got what it takes to convince them and that's all you have to do...and, get on the graveyard shift."

I knew I could use the money. What did I have to lose? Besides, it was just talking. The whole thing seemed pretty harmless.

"Well, okay. I could use the money. There's only one problem. I'll have to sign the card for the other union. If I don't sign it, the foreman won't change my shift. And, I assume you don't want him to know."

"No problem Tom, sign it. Well, y' know what we expect of you...so do a good job. Vincent, here, will show you the ropes...tell you what to say at the shop...that kind of thing."

The big man's arm wound around my shoulder as he stuffed some bills into my jacket unexpectedly. I was a little shocked.

"Thanks, John. I'll try my best. More than my best."

"That's good enough for me. Let's go back to the hall. Only, Tom, from now on let me do the talkin' in there, and remember, this conversation never took place."

The Big Man and Vincent both shook my hand. It was the unwritten agreement that we were now allies.

We re-entered the hall amidst laughter and unrestrained talking. Apparently, in our absence, other speakers had taken over and the tension created by challenging the Big Man was gone. I realize now what the first union lesson was that day. If someone blocks you from your goal, you either take him along for the ride or you eliminate him.

They had gotten me to go along for the ride.

CHAPTER 3

▼

LOOKING FORWARD

Chapter Three

The rest of the evening at the meeting went smoothly, and by the end of the night most of the workers were on our side (I had a side now). I was elated when I arrived at the shop the next morning. I felt like the cat cornering the mouse, my foreman. I had rehearsed my planned conversation with him while dressing, over breakfast, and on my way to work. I went over and over all the ideas I was to plant at the shop. It was going to be easier than I thought.

"Bill, I'm sorry. I left yesterday and forgot to give you this signed card."

"Thanks, Tom. I wasn't worried in the least."

"Bill, are you still short a man on the graveyard shift? If you don't mind, I'd like to change my hours."

"Yeah, we still need someone. That would solve a lot of problems for me...Okay...finish your shift today, and come in tomorrow night at twelve."

Piece of cake. Now I could start my secret mission. I felt like a top level, undercover spy. During the day I kept alert for any useful information. The general topic of the workers' conversations was the union, the union, the union...

Seven men were on my shift. Two, I gathered, were traveling with the boss, three were undecided or just plain tight-lipped, and the other two didn't want any union at all. One thing for sure, no one seemed especially happy. Now it was my turn. All I had to do was drop a few hints designed to explode like bombs in their brains. They were my first targets. During lunch I talked with my shift. Inevitably, our conversation drifted to the union...

Jim, one of the oldest mechanics at the shop, was sitting near me and started the conversation.

"Tom whattaya think of all this? I never in my life thought I'd see the day...being forced to join something you know hardly anything about. Seems that a company union is a bad thing. I don't like it, but what the hell can one man do about it?"

I sat quietly.

"Well, Tom?"

"One man," I said calmly and casually, "can do nothing. He can't do a damn thing. One man is like a match stick. You can break him in two—easy! But take four or five match sticks in your hand and hold them together…and you can't break them. We must band together and make one united decision. Then you'll know what you have."

"I'll tell you, there's something in unity…in unity there's strength. I don't like this idea of a union any more than you do, but we know that one union or another will eventually control this shop. You can see the signs all over the place. Yesterday was just the tip of the iceberg.

"I say, as long as we have to make a choice, we might as well decide which union is best for us. Once we make the right decision and not the boss, then we should band together and demand we get our way!"

"That's good thinking, Tom," Mike said, poking in his own two cents. "But, just how do we go about finding out which union is the one we want controlling things?"

My brain grabbed the word "control" as something clicked upstairs. Now I could throw my next punch, but careful, Tom, slow, play dumb a little, don't let anyone suspect your motives. "Let me tell you somethin'," We don't want a union to control us. We want a union who'll work and fight for us. If we get extra benefits through a union it should be because we deserve them. We work hard and we know our work. We're the best at what we do. I know one thing about this union the boss wants, it's gonna work hard for him, and do just that, control us."

"You're right, Tom. It's just gonna help the boss."

"Yeah, Tom. This union thing should be for us. We're the ones who work the hardest."

"It should be a union for US, working for US, not the boss!"

We talked and talked…union, union, union!… It wasn't long before I realized that I began to sway their train of thought to my side, MY UNION! I also knew that some were acquainted with workers on the other shifts. Did I…could I…start a chain reaction?

You bet! I only had to convert one worker at a time, and urge him to continue my presentation. One domino after another, and suddenly others would start dropping my little bombshells in all the workers' ears. Favoritism towards my union would begin, link by link, and the chain of unity would be strung together, soldered tight.

"Like I said, in unity there's strength. We have to all join together…the few of us here, who don't like what's going on…and, I bet there are more workers all over the place that feel the same way."

"Y' know," said Jim, "I bet there are too. I used to work that other shift last year. Maybe I can run into some of those fellows...see if they'd like to join us for a chat."

"I bet we could get this union thing going. Hell, if we get enough of the others in on the truth here, we could practically run this shop."

"If we get enough men with us, we could walk out, and If they can't operate the machines, we could get the union we want."

"Hey, a strike could also shut down the roadways. Nothin' could come in or out. That would be real power!"

"That's good, Jim. Let's work on this."

"But hell, Tom. We're just day dreaming. Everyone already signed their cards."

"The cards don't mean a damn thing, Mike. Signing 'em was just for show. You could sign a hundred cards and it doesn't hold you responsible for anything. Those cards only mean the union represents the shop, not controls it."

"Are you sure, Tom?"

"Look, no one can force you to do anything that you don't want to. This is America, remember that. All you have to do is talk to everyone you know here. See if they want the boss's union or a better deal with our union. Let me know what they say. Send them to me and I'll talk to 'em."

"Alright. Let's go talk to 'em and get to work. I'll let you know what some of the others think and wanna do."

"Me, too!"

My mind was spinning. One shift...one half of a day's worth of talking...one lunch time's conversing...and I might have half of the workers on my side soon, my union's side. I began to make notes. A little report for Vincent would sure make me shine. Maybe I'd even get another bonus for such fast work.

I literally bounced all over the place. I thought about the graveyard shift that I was starting tomorrow and the two workers there. They were the next two ripe tomatoes waiting to be picked. Piece of cake again. Make you a bet, they didn't like the idea of a company, boss union either.

I was clever, convincing and very persuasive. I finished work feeling the world was my oyster. Here finally was something I could really do. I started to leave the shop and as I stepped onto the street I ran smack into Vincent.

"Success, Vincent! I bet I have over half the men here on our side already. Here are some of my notes."

"Good work, Tom! You haven't wasted any time, and that's something we can't afford to lose. Now, here's what's next on the agenda. I want you to get all the workers in your department to come to another meeting. In fact, make it dinner. Invite 'em all to dinner at our expense at Charlie's Bar and Grill. It's downtown. And don't take no for an answer. You just get 'em there and we'll do the rest!"

"You name it, you got it, Vincent!"

"And Tom call me Vinnie for Christ Sake."

I finally returned home, two flights up to my two rooms. Sometimes, I still thought of the family I had lost and my apartment looked it. It was stark, more like a boarding house set of rooms than a home. Well, maybe this would be just temporary. I usually came home dead tired, ready to hit the sack, so I didn't have much chance to feel my loneliness. Hell, the stove was rarely used but the refrigerator was always filled, at least with beer.

But today was different. I felt I could have thrown a party. And, for a special toast, Jack Daniels, it was. I already was going over my next assignment and rehearsing my lines for the next few days. The adrenalin in my bloodstream was pumping...if it wasn't for the drinks, I might never had gotten to sleep.

It took a couple of days to get the men to the dinner invitation. Out of sixteen, eleven workers showed up. That was a pretty good turn out and I figured I done a great job! The Big Man was there, Vinnie, Mike...

The Big Man did most of the talking. His voice was like velvet, soft and smooth, as he convinced the men that his union was the best for them.

"I want to thank you all for coming," the Big Man started out with orchestrating his sweet, sweet song. "This is gonna be the best thing you ever did! I can get you the best benefits...let my union work for YOU for a change. After all, you work hard for a living...now let someone else work hard for you! You deserve it!

"And, I'm not just talkin' about signing a bunch of cards...I want you to be the first in on this...if you vote us in, I'm gonna give you a free vacation even. I will pay...yes, I said, pay...each and every one of you at least seven dollars a day if we strike...face it, a FREE SEVEN DOLLARS A DAY and you won't even have to walk the line...

"You have the power...if you stop workin', no one else will oppose you. No machinists, no machines. No machines, no shop. Your boss will have to sign up with us just to stay open. It's just that simple...and no, no, your boss won't retaliate...that's what you have us for. We'll even negotiate a "can't get fired rule" without a board investigation first. We'll make sure that no one ever loses a job, especially for striking and fighting for your own, God-given rights.

"Whattaya say? We can do anything. You are the kingpins here. Not your overpaid boss. You're the ones with all the power, and my union has the muscle. Can we vote on this with a show of hands? You leave everything to us and I'll have your boss eatin' out of your hands. Say, YES. Vote our union in, and vote to stay out of the shop. Say, YES."

And believe it or not, they voted unanimously for his union and a shut down! If the machines couldn't produce, the shop would grind to a halt! The shop would have to sign up to stay open. It really was that simple!

The picket line was walking in an orderly fashion. That was good...no loud jeering, no fighting. In fact, no attempt was even made to stop the few that crossed the line. Just a little name-calling and cat-calls. Some of the picketers called the ones crossing the line, "scabs". The police and the union reps just stood around. It looked like it was going to be a quiet day.

And I made the easiest three hundred and fifty dollars ever and was on the road again to something better! What would be my next assignment? How much did the Big Man like me? Would I glide further up their ladder? How much money do you think I could get? Maybe they'll hire me again...was there sunshine today? You bet, there was! Something I hadn't had in quite awhile...I looked forward...

CHAPTER 4

▼

RUDE AWAKENING

Chapter Four

I had been in such a slump for so long…imagine, three hundred and fifty dollars, made so fast and easy, together with another extra seventy-five a week? I liked the sound of big money. This union work is where I really should be. And, just as I had hoped, the Big Man did approach me again.

Vinnie met me leaving the shop one morning.

"Let's get some breakfast," he said. "I know a quiet, little diner…John wants to talk to you."

"Okay."

We drove about twenty minutes, then stopped somewhere down in SoHo. It was the old fashioned kind of diner, opened twenty-four hours a day, with breakfast and luncheon specials, bar with stools, the works. John was already there and had taken a window booth in the back.

"Tom, Tom, sit down…you're doin' such great work for us. I'm so glad to see you."

"Same here, John…yeah, I feel really good…y' know, this is just the kind of thing I've always wanted to do."

"I'm glad to hear you say that…here, order what you want…it's all on me…or, should I say the union?…You can continue working in this shop if you want, but we'd like you to join up with us full-time. Whattaya say?"

"Full time?…Whattaya have in mind?"

"We could really use a man like you. You're a man who knows his trade, inside and out, and that's a point in your favor and ours. We can place you as a worker in any shop we plan to deal with…interested?"

"You mean you can actually get me a job elsewhere? Just like that?"

"Well, because you're a number one mechanic, no one will be suspicious. And, because you are friendly, people warm up to you easily…and you talk well. This will benefit us both.

"We'll give you a hundred and twenty-five a week over whatever the shop gives you. Once you're there, you do just what you did at your old shop. You just talk, persuade…plant a few good rumors about the union. Get 'em to join our union. And if the workers feel you are one of 'em, they're more apt to be influenced by you. Well, Tom, that's the deal. Whattaya say? Wanna join us?"

"Hell, that sounds good enough for me. I have nothing to lose. You're right, I do like to talk to people, and I like the excitement. Yeah, this could prove to be an interesting job. Alright, I'm in. Now what's my next move? What's the next shop?"

"I'm glad you're in...now to business. We got a job all lined up for you. There's a shop over in Raritan that we want, and with your help we're gonna get it."

"It's a small place with no more than fifty people working there. They need a mechanic and I want you to go get that job...make it the night shift! Mike will work with you and show you what we want. Oh, by the way, we rented a room for you out there. Mike will show you where it is. And another thing, run up an expense account, if you need to."

"What the hell do you mean I have a room out there? Were you so sure I would take the job?"

"To tell you the truth, Tom, yes. I was almost certain you would. I know an enterprising man when I see one. Your type doesn't throw away opportunity."

"What about my apartment here in town? Can't I commute back and forth?"

"I thought it would be easier on you. But do what you want. That's entirely up to you. Just let Mike know."

He got out of his chair, took my hand and shook it, padding mine with some bills.

"I won't be seeing much of you, but I'll be in touch. All I can say is good luck. Stay in touch with Mike and Vinnie."

I drove out to the Raritan shop the next day. Two young fellows, Jack and Jim, were running the place and they were very cordial towards me. Getting the job was easy. Piece of cake again! It seemed they were in desperate need of a mechanic and I did know the job, inside and out. We became friends almost immediately.

I was placed on the day shift for a while so they could keep an eye on me, and see if I really knew my trade. I didn't blame them. In the wrong hands, these machines could break down and cause expensive repairs. Everything went fine. It wasn't long before I started on the night shift, which is where I originally wanted to be.

Mike asked me to snoop first. He handed me a list of information to look for...buyers, truckers used, shipping schedules, suppliers, names and addresses of all the workers.

This was a non-union shop with only two shifts, twelve hours each. Only two other men were on my night shift, each of us operating five machines at the same time. It turned out that these men didn't know much about who they were manufacturing merchandise for. And, there was no one else around during the night to ask or bullshit with.

Some information I was able to track through the orders I handled. However, Mike told me it was taking too long and that the data wasn't always accurate. I decided I could bullshit some of it, but I still had to get information another way. I had to get into the office somehow.

I found out the office wasn't locked at night, but it was hard to find a way to spend a lot of time there without creating suspicion. I had located the books and started collecting my information, but it was going too slowly. Well, you can only go to the bathroom so many times.

Then I hit upon an idea! Why not use the phone in the office? If I used the phone during my break what better reason did I have to be there?

Mike and I worked out for a girl to call me every night. To everyone else, for a week straight, I received a phone call from my girl friend who was the chatterbox. The calls would last fifteen minutes or so. That gave me plenty of time to be snooping and writing down the information I was looking for. In fact, this worked out so well that checking in with my girl got to be a standard gag around the shop.

Meanwhile, union talk began to get passed around. Mike told me that about twenty workers had signed their cards already. One day, I was delayed at the shop because the man who usually relieved me had car trouble. When he finally got to the shop, it was about seven AM. I walked out surprisingly into a picket line, and recognized many of the people from my union—Connie, Jane, Jack...even Mike was there. I pretended not to know them and walked to my car. As I opened the door I saw Vinnie sitting there, next to the driver's seat.

"Hi, Tom! Hop in." he said.

"What's up?" I said.

"Let's get some coffee."

I drove around the corner to a diner, and we went inside and settled ourselves in a booth.

"How's it going, Tom?"

"Alright. Mike has my full report. I've given him practically everything he asked for. How come the picket line? I wasn't told about it."

"We heard from a rat that another union is getting ready to throw their hooks into this shop, so we decided to move up our time table. We wanted to beat 'em to it by throwing up our line first. Now, how are the mechanics gonna vote? Are they with us or against?"

"Against us," I said. "The majority don't approve of any union. Anyways, I like 'em a helluva lot. Let 'em be content, they're regular guys."

Vinnie looked at me peculiarly.

"Let's go sit in the car, Tom. I wanna talk to you privately about something."

I was expecting a lecture in the car. Instead, it was a rude awakening.

"Tom, I'm gonna be straight with you. And you better fuckin' listen and fuckin' listen good. This is a tough, not always pleasant racket. There's no room for sentiment in this type of work. You haven't been fuckin' hired to like anyone. You do as you're told. I don't care how important someone may be to you or how much you fuckin' like 'em...don't. And, I mean, don't."

"I've been doing alright so far," I countered. "I haven't ever refused to follow any of your orders. And you know that. So I said Jack and Jim are good bosses, but that doesn't mean anything really. I'm a union man now, and when I'm assigned a job I'll do it. Don't you worry, Vinnie, I'm with you."

"Okay, Tom, we'll see. I'm convinced we're gonna have a rough time getting into your shop, and we haven't much time to waste. So I have no alternative. Here's what I want you to do. There are fifteen machines in the shop, but four of them are really important. If those four machines were to magically break down...Do you get it?"

"You must be kidding? You want me to wreck those machines, just like that? Do you realize what it would cost to repair somethin' like that? Why, it wouldn't be fair to Jack or Jim."

Vinnie raised his voice and his fist towards me. I almost belted him one too.

"GOD DAMN IT, Tom, listen to me. We want our fuckin' union in this shop and we don't care how the hell we get there. Regardless of the methods we use, we're gonna control that shop. Look, Tom, you're making over a hundred a week with us. We pay for your room and your expenses. What'll Jack and Jim say if they found out? What would your old shop boss do, if he found out you were in on that picket line and that shut down?

"That's pretty good fuckin' money you're making with us. If you want to keep hearing the sound of it, you're gonna have to change your sentimental, pussy thinking. I never said you were always gonna be Mr. Nice guy here.

"If you want to stay with us then you have to get rid of, throw all your sentimental feelings away. You're gonna have to toughen up, or we don't need you. Would you like to take a little walk right now?…

I didn't say anything. I knew what "a little walk" could mean. He could get rid of me. Think, Tom…keep your cool. This guy was muscling me.

"When you work for the union," Vinnie continued in a nasty tone, "it's the survival of the fittest. If you ain't fit to play the game, don't be a player. You're either with us all the way, or you're out…which way will it be?"

Vinnie pulled out a gun.

CHAPTER 5

▼

MACHINES BLOW

Chapter Five

A gun has a script of its own. I did nothing except freeze. Vinnie lowered his voice.

"I'm the one that brought you in, Tom. My ass is on the line, right now. We're paying you a lot of fuckin' money and we need that shop to justify it. I'm sure I won't have to do anything further to persuade you…Right?"

I didn't answer for a while, just stared through the car's window shield. Not even a million thoughts ran through my mind. It was blank. I was in shock.

Come on, Tom, don't be so naive. You always knew somewhere in the back of your stupid head that they played dirty. What did you think? They just pushed a button and everyone signed a card with smiles, and all the bosses just happily accepted and signed the contracts?

Come on Tom, you knew what was what when you once saw someone suddenly disappear…a troublemaker, without a trace. Do you want to be next?

"Okay, Vinnie…don't get so hot under the collar. I told you, I'm in."

"Go home, Tom. I'll tell John that you said your in. It's the only way."

He patted me on the shoulder and smelled of the devil. I needed a drink.

I didn't go home right away. Why did I have the funny feeling that I was being watched? That guy was making me paranoid. But, those union guys had a funny way of knowing your whereabouts. They knew my work schedule. They knew where I lived. The only thing, thank God, they didn't know, was about my kids.

Sitting there in the tavern with my favorite Jack Daniels, I started pounding out the questions. This was going to be the turning point in my life, wasn't it? If I backed out, wouldn't they hurt me? Didn't I know too much already? I met too many faces already, faces that would not tolerate the lime light.

Then, again, perhaps this was just Vinnie's problem. I really didn't know him well. Maybe his congenial facade was just a cover for someone who really likes to muscle people. Or, maybe he was just kidding. No, this one meant business. He would hurt me. I didn't have any choice.

And, the money. I liked the money. It was like a habit already. The shop's salary was only a drop in the bucket. Why the hell should I be obligated to them? So I liked Jack and Jim. A man can only have one boss. I joined the union of my own free will…well, maybe the money had something to do with it. And I knew from the war, you have to take orders. The boss gives the orders and I had to obey.

This is just how it's going to be. Just do this one thing once, Tom, and you can always just pull out and leave. At least no one is going to get hurt. It's just a God damn machine, isn't it? They probably have insurance...so why sweat, Tom?

Okay, downing my third drink, I'll do it. Should ask for more money though. This is more riskier than just snooping through mail and files and copying down information.

In the beginning, I thought...or wanted to believe...this was a clean business, like my old store. But didn't I scalp some of the customers when I knew they could afford it? Didn't I keep some of the cash back and not pay all the taxes? So clean, huh, Tom?

Don't be so naive. I have to recognize every aspect of the union in its true light. And, I'm not the one to turn down big money. Whenever they toss an order in my lap, I must convince myself it's my job and I have to carry it out. It has to be this way or not at all. I must accept it.

I wanted the glamor of working for the union, didn't I? I wanted the job to be plenty active and filled with thrills and excitement. Well, to pull this off and not get caught will be plenty exciting. If you're afraid of the danger involved in the job, you're afraid of yourself. Don't be such a pussy Tom.

Was this the fourth or fifth shot of whiskey? Who cares? My conscience felt muddled...then I felt better. Instead of wrestling with my low resistance to this job...hell, I'll throw you, my emotions and sentiments out the window. That's just what Vinnie wants anyway so there will be no problem. When it comes to the union, I can take it or leave it. I'll do it...it's that simple.

I went to the pay phone and phoned Mike.

"Yeah, this is Mike. Make it quick."

"Hi, Mike, this is Tom."

"Oh, hi, Tom. Is this gonna take long? Did Vin talk to ya?"

"Yeah, he talked to me. It's no big deal, I just wanted you and John to know. I know exactly how to handle this. But, I'm gonna need an extra envelope. It's much, more riskier, you know. Can you take care of that?"

"Yeah, I'll talk to John and get back to you."

"Okay. Tell John, thanks."

Click went the phone line. I still couldn't believe I was going through with this. My hand was actually shaking. Damn it, Tom. Get hold of yourself.

Did I cross over an invisible line after hanging up the phone? And once over this line, would I ever be able to retrace my footsteps back again? Was this a never looking back…a permanent entanglement in the union's web?

When I arrived home, I found someone had slipped an envelope under the doorway. Five hundred dollars and I almost pissed my pants. Someone was anxious about something. I guess I had to kill the machines as soon as possible. First another drink and some sleep.

I was too exhausted, especially mentally, to even take off my clothes. I decided to concentrate on the how to's of my present assignment or I would be up all night wrestling again with right and wrong. I drifted slowly into sleep and began to see the whole thing laid up. They were right, I was a top mechanic. Probably the best one to know how to fix everything.

Upon waking, I rehearsed the job. The machines had to be destroyed. It wouldn't be easy, but it wasn't so impossible. Funny how money makes you feel better in the morning. I was actually looking forward to planning the whole thing now.

I needed the opportunity to approach the machines, the key ones, when they were unattended. Seemed a remote possibility since one of the mechanics was always there. In the event a machine broke down, you had to answer to the boss. If it was through neglect or misuse, there would be hell to pay. In fact, I, like the other mechanics, would never let anyone near my machines during my shift.

So, I had to fix them when they were unattended. There was a time when the machines were idle and the place vacant and that was on Fridays. Most Fridays, the boys and I took our break together and went to a local bar for a few beers and a bite to eat.

So it was settled. No more conscience pangs and the great taste of money in my mouth. I deserved it. When Gus and Otto went to the bar on Friday, I would just say I was tired and wanted to grab a little nap. After that, I would wait about ten minutes to make sure the coast was clear. I would take out my bagged lunch, but instead of lunch, inside would be sand. Pure sand, that would do it. That's all it would take to wreck the damn machines.

"Coming with us, Tom?"

"No. I didn't get enough sleep last night, think I'll take a short nap. Wake me when you get back, okay?"

"Do you want us to bring you back anything?"

"No, no. That's okay. I bagged it again," I said as I nestled down in my chair, hat over my eyes, glancing slightly at my watch for ten minutes to slide by.

I fetched the small bag from my lunch pail and approached the closest machine. Then, very carefully and slowly, I started pouring the sand in the small oil holes of the machine. I switched the motor on for a minute or two and let the machine spin a few turns. After cleaning off the excess sand, I repeated the same operation with the remaining machines, including my own...then flushed the leftover sand in the toilet.

When the men returned to the shop, I pretended to be asleep. Gus woke me up by the shoulder and we went back to work.

I knew that the sand would gradually mix with the oil in the machines...then cause a binding reaction, causing them to stop completely. I also figured that it would take more than three hours for this reaction to begin. I was wrong on both points.

The first surprise came a little before two hours had elapsed. All hell broke loose. The two machines Gus was operating, kicked into a mess first. One stopped working completely and as Gus was trying to find out what gone wrong, the other machine split its cam in two, screeching to a halt. As I turned to Otto, his expression of surprise turned to fright as he dove to the floor trying to escape the flying metal blasting all over the shop.

I only had time for a fleeting glance at him, when my own machine began rumbling and I knew it was ready to blow. I hit the floor with a crashing thud, but not fast enough.

A searing pain hit my lungs as a jagged piece of metal dug into my back. I hugged the floor and kept my head down. Pressing my hand to my back I felt the warm, sticky flow of blood and wondered how could I have misjudged everything? The pain became more severe, and I began to curse and swear, damning everyone before lapsing into unconsciousness. It was dark and I don't think I even dreamed.

CHAPTER 6

▼

THREE DAYS IN LOVE

Chapter Six

I don't know how much time had passed as I became aware of my surroundings. The noise had subsided and I tried to raise myself weakly from the floor.

The room was in shambles. At least five machines had been rendered useless, windows were broken everywhere, and a small fire had started in one corner. Otto was trying to put it out and, as I started towards him, a spinning sensation caught me. The next thing I heard was the thud of my own body as I hit the floor, unconscious again.

I opened my eyes to a room of confusion and people. Police, firemen, my bosses, everyone seemed there. I spotted Jack and guilt and remorse began to slither inside me only to be blotted out by the severe pain I was in. I turned my dizzy head and ended up against a white jacket. Suddenly, I realized it was a doctor who was probing my back injury.

"What the hell are you, a horse doctor?" I shouted. "Take it easy."

"How's it going Tom?" Jack asked, his eyes filled with tears. "You have a nasty gash there. Do you feel up to talking? Can you remember anything that happened?"

"How the hell should I know? I was just standing near my machine one minute and the next thing I knew someone is jabbing my back. It happened so fast."

I tried to get up. I wanted to get the hell out of there, away from Jack's sad eyes, so full of compassion for me. The doctor's hand said no to that.

"Quiet son, don't get so excited. Some metal cut your back. Looks like a nasty gash."

"Doc, I don't have insurance. Can't you just patch it up?"

"If you want me to dress it properly, you'll have to lie quietly for a while. Here, on your side, you'll feel more comfortable. Let me give you some shots, and see what I can do."

"It'll take more than that to keep me down, doc."

The police were questioning Gus and Otto, but they knew nothing. They questioned me but it didn't seem there would be an investigation. No one suspected foul play. I felt very guilty. Everyone was so kind to me. Ironic, wasn't it? The only one who was injured was me. Guess I deserved it.

Jack wanted me to take some time off, even offered to give me some severance pay, whatever he could afford. I insisted I would be in shape to work in a couple of days. He even was reluctant to let me drive myself home, but I stubbornly refused his assistance. The doc had patched me up just fine and the pain killer had kicked in. I just couldn't wait to get out of there.

As I neared my car, I spotted Mike. Boy, that guy just always knew when I was leaving, and this time, I wasn't in the mood. He quickly matched my stride, keeping about four to five feet away, and lowered his voice.

"Just keep walking...so it doesn't look like we're talking...Jesus, Tom, we didn't say wreck the joint. What the hell happened? By the way, great work."

"Listen, Mike, just leave me the hell alone. I almost got killed in there tonight."

"Easy, easy. You did fine. John never forgets good work. When you reach your car...look under the hood. He asked me to give ya another two hundred dollars. In case you had medical expenses."

"I'm just completely out of this one Mike I didn't expect to get hurt."

"I need to know if anyone suspects anything? Did the police talk to you?"

"I'm not in the mood for questions now, Mike, but no, no one knows. I'm free to go."

"You want me drive you home?"

"No, no. You'll get my report. Can I go now?" I said with much irritation.

"Yeah, Go home and rest. I'll call ya later."

"Yeah, yeah...make that a big later. I'm takin' a few sick days...'til I'm feeling better."

"Wanna grab a drink?"

"Yeah, my Jack Daniels is waiting for me at home...now, get lost already...before someone sees us."

Booze, I thought, reaching for my flask. Good old John. The money was right where Mike said it would be. My back began to throb as I drove myself home. I was filled with anger and hate. I hated my back, I hated the pain, I hated the union, my job, I hated, just plain period, hated. I must have drunk about six straight shots before I finally made it home to collapse.

I awoke with ringing in my ear. I reached for the phone but there was no one on the line. The ringing continued. This was a hell of a hangover I thought until I realized it was the doorbell. I glanced at the clock and realized that most of the day had gone by. I wasn't in the mood for company, but whoever it was, was determined to get the door open.

"Hi, Tom. How'da you feel?" were their first words.

It was Vinnie, Mike, Connie, Jane, and Jean, all from the union.

"Someone sure looks like he slept in his clothes."

"Leave me alone. I'm very tired, and need a painkiller."

"Oh come on, Tom. We wanna help you celebrate."

They wanted to celebrate. I had destroyed a man's place of business accidentally, practically got myself killed, and these bastard's were happy about it. On top of it all, they wanted to celebrate.

I was going to lift the back of my shirt and show them the great, little gash I had to celebrate, but Connie, cute little Connie, turned my anger around.

"Were you hurt bad? Let me see. You just sit down here and relax," she said so sweetly that I just followed her instructions without protest. Everyone else started to grin.

"Don't mind them, honey," she said as she gently brushed my shirt away from my wound. I suddenly realized I had forgotten about the pain and was only mesmerized by the sweet touch of her fingertips against my skin.

"Wow, that's a beauty. But, it doesn't look infected. Let me change the dressing for you. Bandages in there? What'd they use, a bomb?" Connie and her tender touch...I only had to look at her from a distance as her hips brushed past me, and I was already lost somewhere in a fantasy.

"The shop's ready to sign with us, Tom," Mike said. "You shouldn't worry. They had insurance and they'll be operational in about two weeks. You did such a good job."

"Let's have some fun and celebrate."

"I don't know guys. Suppose someone spots us? Wouldn't it look funny for me to be celebrating after my accident."

"Who the hell cares Tom. You get two good shops signed up in just one month and all you wanna do is just sit there. Come on let's celebrate and stop feeling sorry for yourself. We need better men, like him, don't we, Connie?"

"You should be happy that your becoming a good earner, exactly what John wants. Pretty soon any job you do will be easy. Shake it off, Tom. Go get a fresh shirt. Connie wants to go out with you tonight, right Connie?"

My glance went towards Connie and I was more than satisfied with the view. I eyed her again, from her encouraging eyes down past her nice, low cut dress.

"Okay," I finally said. "Just give me some time to shave and change. I'll meet you at Bromfields...is that where we're going?"

"I'll wait for you here, Tom," Connie said, settling down comfortably in a chair as she motioned the others out of the apartment.

"Bromfields, it is. Don't the two of you take too long…"

"Okay…Connie, can you make me a drink? I'll be ready soon."

I turned to look at her. The hell of the shop and the still throbbing pain in my back slipped away again. All I could think about was Connie…Connie's sweet smile, her soft voice, her cute, proportioned figure, those provocative, upturned breasts, and that enticing fire in her eyes. In those eyes I read an invitation and was secretly glad the others had gone.

She came over to me with our drinks and draped her arm around me gently. I pulled her towards me.

"We don't have to join them, if you don't want to, y' know?…"

"I know…but, won't they be upset…how about we just catch up with 'em for a little while? We don't have to spend the whole night with 'em exactly."

I watched her again. She melted into the apartment, into the furnishings somehow as if she was meant to be there. As if she always had been there. As I said, in those eyes, in that figure, the way she moved across the floor, hips swaying slightly, there was an invitation…funny, it was the first time in a long time I didn't think about my deceased wife.

Connie and I finally arrived at the club.

"You two, sure took a long time. Celebrating before you got here? Here, we just ordered."

"Ready and willing," I replied. "Let's eat and have some fun."

As the band played, I leaned over toward Connie and asked her if she wanted to dance. We walked out to the dance floor, and in my arms, she seemed to melt like butter. She was the fragrance of intoxication, and the softness and warmth of her body…as I held her close, overwhelmed me.

"You're so beautiful," I said. She didn't answer so I stepped back to gaze at her, looking straight into her big, blue eyes burning with even more fire.

"Let's go somewhere."

"Alright," she whispered.

The eyes that met mine that night were filled with desire and passion. As I held out my arms, she slipped into my soul, our lips touching, then our bodies. She was all that I wanted and even more…the softest skin and breasts so tender to my touch…I fondled her and caressed her for hours it seemed as the fire in her eyes transferred into her body. It was difficult to believe there could be so much passion in one person.

Three days went by. Night and day, day and night we were together, but to tell you the truth, I had no idea what day it was. We sent in for food and took the phone off the hook. Even when she left the room, her smell was everywhere with me.

Then, suddenly, the aroma of freshly brewed coffee awoke me. It was quiet, too quiet.

"Connie?...Connie?"

There was no answer and I knew she was gone. For three beautiful days of joy I felt all the tension built up inside of me slowly slip away. Peace of mind and tranquility arrived like moonlight on a summer night...shining...breaking through the darkness of my life.

Connie was something I needed and wanted. She was wonderful...why did it end?

Although a good-bye had not passed between us, I expected to find a note. There was nothing on the kitchen table, but I knew she had left, just the same. Only her reflection remained...her smell, still everywhere, overwhelmed the coffee's aroma as I saw her image drift through my mind. It was no dream, but it was dreamlike, sipping my coffee, and then hearing her suddenly in the bathroom, jarring me into consciousness.

I was wrong. She had not left. Thank God! Strange and beautiful...this woman.

CHAPTER 7

▼

NEW PARTNER

Chapter Seven

I walked up the stairs to the office.

"Hi, Pat! John in?"

"Hi, Tom. Yes, he's in his office. Go right in...he's expecting you."

John stood up as I entered his office, grabbing me with a strong, warm handshake.

"Hello, Tom. How are things? That was a fuckin' beautiful job. I'm proud of you. I knew you had it in you."

"Thanks. I'm fine. In fact, superb today. Here's my report. I'll always follow orders."

"Looking good, Tom. Mike and I were a little fuckin' worried there, but I see you're okay now. Glad you got it off your chest. And, how is Connie? You two seem to be quite an item."

I laughed inside. It was a set-up, wasn't it? They think they planned the whole Connie thing. Guess they didn't know what a great lover I was. Was I supposed to thank them. Well, what they don't know won't hurt them. What "assholes". Let them think what they want.

"Thanks for the money, John. I could really use it...Connie? Wow, a real sweetheart. I had a feeling you were behind us meeting. Thanks for that too."

"I'm glad things took for you, Tom. She's a nice lady. We all felt you were under too much pressure, that you needed a break. Well, it worked. You look relaxed and happy...now, let's get down to business. I've got a new assignment for you."

"What?"

"We have a strike going on in Butler and I'm givin' you the job. You'll work with Salvatore (Sallie) Toccola. Ever meet him before?"

"No. can't say I have."

"Pat? Can you send Sal in? Tom, you listen to Sallie and follow his orders. He's the best. He's well educated with union rules and been with us for a long time, you'll learn a lot from him."

"Great."

Sallie walked in. He was tall in stature, about six feet three, solid and muscular...but somehow, his brown wavy hair, the tender expression on his face, and his gentle smile didn't fit. Deceptive somehow.

"Sallie, close the door, have a seat. This is your new partner, Tom Furcco."

"Glad to meet ya, Tom."

"Same here, Sallie. John told me you're the best."

There were two phones on John's desk. One started to ring, the black one.

"I have to take this call. Sallie, take Tom across the street for a drink."

John swivelled his chair and waited for us to leave before answering the phone. Secrets. I had never seen him use that phone until today. But this information I wasn't in on...yet.

Sallie and I left the union office together and walked across the street to the tavern. He selected a booth farthest from the busy bar area, in the back.

"I'm gonna outline the whole deal for you. Have you ever been on a picket line?"

"Not really. I usually spy for John from inside the shop. Get a job there first. That kind of thing."

"Well, it's not so hard if you just want to make a public statement. But if you're told to keep all the workers and anyone else from crossing the line, it can be messy. You know how to fight?"

"Yeah. Saw a lot of action in the army. Five years. I'd say I can handle myself."

"Well, if you have to use violence, use your head first. Then your hands and feet, punching and kicking. If you have to use a weapon, don't get pinched. Use it and get rid of it. And watch for the cops. If they see you, then it's assault. They'll take you in. Just don't get pinched.

"Now, at this Butler plant, we have a beef with this other union that's trying to get in. We have about the same number of workers on the picket line as they have working in the plant. We threw up a picket line and ran it in an orderly fashion, but their group keeps crossing. We kept a few from entering the shop, but not everyone. John didn't want us to use force yet.

"Then, things got ugly. A bunch of goons mingled with the workers one morning and crashed the line. They came with baseball bats, shovels, two by fours, and even picks, and they really hit us hard. We almost broke up and a few of our crew got broken legs and arms.

"It seems that the other union has the police in their pocket, because they teamed up. That's what it looks like...makes it twice as difficult."

"Yeah, now you have two sides to deal with. The police, huh? That's not good."

"So we're gonna have a tough fight on our hands. We'll have to make the line stronger. Anything and anyone must be stopped from entering the shop.

This is why you've been assigned to me. Hey, look at the time. Let's get outta here. We'll have dinner at my house. Then, we'll stay at your place tonight…you're closer to Butler. You got a couch or something for me?"

"Yeah, I got a sofa bed," I answered a little hesitantly.

"Tom, this is how it has to be. We have to live, eat, and stay together for about a week or so. It's the only way. You have a lot to learn, and in order for me to take you under my wing and teach you how things are done in this business, I have to be with you at all times. I don't want anything to go wrong. Okay?"

"Okay, by me. We can share everything if that's what you want—except, of course, our women."

"Tom, the first thing you have to learn is there are no women. We don't get involved when we're on the job. I don't even go home. Do you understand?"

"Okay, Sallie. Whatever you say. You're the boss."

"Right now, We're going to my house. My wife knows nothing about me working for a union. What we're involved in cannot be shared with anyone. Not even our wives. She'll just pack a bag for me for a business trip. So, don't let on about anything we've talked about. She's a great cook, by the way."

I was surprised to hear that Sallie was married. And what a beautiful wife and what a beautiful house he had. None of this back alley, out of sight apartment stuff.

I was introduced as a business associate. His wife, Sheila, was wonderful. And, I agreed, a great cook. She treated me like one of the family. As the evening wore on, Sallie really did ask her to pack a bag for him. She didn't protest or question anything. She just went into the bedroom and started packing.

While that was going on, Sallie went into his study and opened up a locked desk drawer. He took out a small case and motioned for me to take it out to the car.

"Nice meeting you, Sheila," I said on the way out. "I'll go wait outside and have a smoke."

"You have a good trip, Tom. Happy to meet you."

Sallie came out in a few minutes, bag in hand, and we drove to my place. When we got settled, I opened a bottle of Jack Daniels and got out a few beers."

"Have you got any tools, Tom?"

"Tools? Whattaya mean?"

"Guns."

"Oh! I have a forty-five. And, a favorite knife. From the war."

"Did you ever kill anyone, Tom?"

"Yeah, I did. During the war."

"Was that the first time?"

"Yep."

"Make you ill at all? Some don't have the stomach for it."

"Yeah. When I killed my first Jap, I was just plain sick. It lasted a long time and I hated myself for a while. But it was kill or be killed. Then I got to see what they did. Horrible things. And that hate got turned around. It became easier to kill. They were just wild animals and I had to eliminate 'em all I could."

"Let me see the gun and knife."

I walked into my bedroom and flipped the switch. My gun and knife were hidden in a hole in the wall behind a picture. The knife's ivory handle glowed almost. It was my prize possession. The blade was nine inches long with a razor sharp edge on both sides."

"Hey, that's a beaut', Tom. Where'd you get it?"

"I took it off a Jap."

My mind wandered back through the years, and I saw myself walking along the island's beach years ago. It was there I had spotted the body of a dead Jap. I wanted a souvenir, so I walked cautiously toward him. When I reached his body, I turned him over on his back. His expressionless eyes looked at me and I could see he wasn't breathing.

He was wearing an expensive looking watch. I took it off his wrist and turned towards the light as it flashed in my hand. It was a beauty and I admired it greatly. I was trying to get the back off to see if it had any gems when I heard a movement behind me.

"There were Japs dead all over the place, Sallie. But one must've played dead. He jumped up from the ground in a cat-like leap behind me and lunged at me. I side stepped and he plunged past me and lost his balance.

"Then he jumped up again as I started raising my gun. He had this knife in his hand. The switch jammed on my carbine. I thought I was gonna die. I swung it at him…caught him in the chest and grabbed his arm so that the knife slipped. Guess you know who survived."

"Yeah. You took it off a Jap alright. Well, let's talk over war stories some other time. I have a few myself, but I'm tired. Let's see the gun."

I handed Sallie the gun and took back my beloved knife, the one that had saved my life.

"This gun is in good shape, Tom, but it's too heavy and awkward. Here take this thirty-two instead."

"Thanks, Sallie...nice, tapered handle and all. Sure you don't mind loaning it? Suppose it gets tossed?"

I had no intention of using it, but, decided to play along. I lingered somewhere in my mind, and thought of Connie.

"Don't worry about it."

"What does your wife have to say about all this Sallie? She never catches on?"

"Sheila thinks I'm a salesman, and that's all she has to know. The union covers for me. We even have a fake number if she tries to call me. The secretary knows how to answer it."

"They think of everything, don't they?"

"You'll see...even though you're single, they'll cover for you too. Just don't be weak and just don't get pinched ever. There'll be no traces. One way or another."

"Can I ask you somethin'?"

"Sure. What?"

"What's with the black phone in John's office?"

"Can't say. He's the only one who ever uses it. Not even his secretary. Keep your nose clean, Tom. Tomorrow's gonna be a long day. I'm turning in. This is a nice place. We should use it more often...I like the location, discreet but convenient...well, we can talk about it later...night..."

"Yeah, good-night, Sallie."

I didn't fall asleep right away. Sallie snored immediately.

CHAPTER 8

▼

THE DEATH LINE

Chapter Eight

As we walked up the street near the plant, everything seemed to be in turmoil. The street was almost impassable. Six squad cars were lined up along the curb and police were all over the place. The picket line was huge and powerful and more than a hundred people were on it. It was still early, but the atmosphere gave me a feeling of impending disaster.

"Tom, I want you to stay in this spot. Don't move. Just watch."

"Okay."

The grim, intense expressions on the maze of faces increased my feeling of dread. Something bad was going to happen soon. I just couldn't shake the feeling that gripped me as I watched.

Suddenly, I heard a roar from the crowd. As I looked towards the corner I saw a group of workers marching on the shop. They were surrounded by a cordon of policemen led by their captain. He shouted to the picket line to disperse, but they refused.

It looked like a cattle stampede. The two lines of people met with the thumping of clubs and blood started to flow everywhere. Faces and fists crashed into each other, that it made me shudder just to watch. Then there was mass hysteria. Anyone who tried to escape was knocked down and trampled. Even the people just standing and watching joined in shouting and throwing fists. I started forward myself.

People were on the ground and needed medical attention...some were women. But union men know how to operate. The picket line remained steady as the marchers began to fall back.

Then the police hit the line with their reserves. It was a blood bath. They grabbed three union men and tried to force them into a squad car. Half of the picket line went for the police and turned the car on its side. Gas spilled from the car and somehow ignited. A woman screamed "fire" and I saw Mike fall to the ground.

I ran towards him and found him unconscious. I grabbed him by the collar and managed to drag him about twenty-five feet when an explosion hit us knocking us down. Someone shrieked as I threw my body over his. Debris was falling all around us.

Then the yells were replaced with moans and cries. Three people near us were lying motionless on the ground. Two more were barely able to get up.

"Mike, are you alright?" I gently turned him on his back and his lifeless eyes stared back at me.

"Mike!" I yelled.

Mike didn't answer and I didn't know if he ever would. Blood flowed from his chest as I saw a knife in it. I pulled it out but it didn't matter. He must have been dead even before I reached him.

Sallie found me crouched, horrified there beside Mike's dead body and pushed me away from the area as everyone began fleeing except for the injured and dead. We ended up in a small, tuck-away bar.

I was speechless for a long time, completely in shock and literally shaking.

"Tom, I feel just the way you do. We all do. We lost a loyal friend. We can't bring him back but we can try like hell to make this up to him."

"You can bet, someone is gonna pay."

"He would've been proud of you…risking your life for him. If I live to be a hundred, I couldn't meet anyone with more balls. Here you turn the tables on me when I'm supposed to be educating you, your educating me. I'm not giving you a sermon, Tom, but you have filled me with so much trust in you…the way you ran to his side and risked your own life. Come on, get out of the fuckin' dumps. Shake it off. Let's have another drink."

His words hit me in the right channels as I began to slowly snap out of it. Sallie placed his hand on my shoulder as he left the table to use the phone. A few minutes later he returned with some news.

"I just talked to John."

"Anyone else get hurt?"

"Connie and Vinnie got pinched."

"Connie?" I snapped.

"Calm down. She isn't hurt and they both should be out on bail in a hour."

"Do you mean to tell me that Connie was mixed up in this mess? She didn't tell me she was assigned to this plant's line."

"She may have been given last minute instructions. Did ya see who knifed Mike?"

"No. It happened too fast."

"Well, I swear we'll go through hell and high water to find out who it was. We always take care of our own beefs."

"If you do, I want him. Leave him to me and my knife. Nice and quiet and with a lot of pain."

"I know, Tom…we'll see. Let's go now. Connie and Vinnie will be waiting for us. The line won't start forming for a while. The place right now is crawling with cops and ambulances."

We met up with them at the union office. I thought about Connie the whole trip in. As soon as I saw her, I looked into her eyes. Her fiery expression changed and she glanced at me in a soft, warm way. The invitation was still there.

"Mike's dead, did John tell you?"

Both Vinnie and Connie looked stunned.

"What the fuck happened?" they both asked at once.

"He was knifed. Tom tried to save him as the patrol car exploded, but he was dead before he could reach him."

"Knife, explosion…we must've been locked up before the shit hit the fan. Can't believe Mike is dead. He's been around here for a long time…a good man. You worked with him for awhile didn't ya, Tom?"

"Yeah, I did. He was a great guy…what happens now Sallie? Who's gonna tell Mike's wife?"

"I can be there if you want," Connie said.

"I'll ask John what he wants. Well, I suggest that everyone go home for now and get some rest. Tomorrow, Tom, you'll be on the line. You know the shit by now. I know you can take care of yourself, just be careful. Don't get pinched like I said before."

"Does she have to be there too?" I asked, pointing to Connie. "If she is, I'll be on double duty, watching the line and watching her."

Connie looked at me with a surprised expression.

"Listen, Tom, I've been on more damn picket lines than you've ever seen, and I can take care of myself. I know what to do, and I don't need you to protect me."

I took Sallie aside.

"I just don't want her to get hurt. You know what you said, no women, no involvements. This is personal and it will get in the way…if y' know what I mean."

"Connie," Sallie turned to her and motioned with his hand, giving her the ax.

"Oh, alright then," she pouted. "If it'll make you feel compromised, I'll take myself off the line," and she stood up to leave, leaning over me to give me a peck on the cheek.

"I'll see YOU later," and off she went.

It must have hurt her deeply to eliminate herself as a worker on the line, but she had, and I was very happy she hadn't put up much of a fuss. I knew she knew…it was because I cared about her.

For the fourth day in a row, the two lines clashed. I was guarding the door that led into the shop. I had my feet astride with my back facing the door. A face loomed in front of me and I smashed my fist into his mouth. "That's for Mike!"

The man started to fall but was pushed away with the rush of the mob. I hit someone else and he fell to the ground. No sooner was he trampled underfoot, then I had to swing at another face, and another, and another.

I was punched, shook it off, and swung again. The crowd became so dense that it was suddenly too hard for me to recognize anything more than a blue blur. I had hit a patrolman. I tried to ward off the club that came crashing down on my skull. I felt the blood streaming down the side of my face and tried to grab out for the club as it descended on me for a second time.

I wrestled, managing to loosen his firm grasp, but as I attempted to hit him I missed. A sharp pain invaded my body as something hit me on the back of the neck. A sinking sensation took hold of me as I felt myself falling into a deep void of darkness.

A voice seemed to be pounding in my ears.

"Tom. Wake up. Drink this."

I felt my eyes open and the liquid seemed to burn clear down to my toes. I almost choked.

"Enough," I said as I sat up. "What happened?"

I was sitting in Sallie's car, and as I looked out the window I expected to see the rioting crowd, but the street was deserted. The state troopers were all lined up with guns drawn keeping the irate mob on the sidewalk. I stared at Sallie, dumbfounded.

"They called in the state troopers. Uncle Sam is taking over. It's just about finished, except for the voting."

"I don't understand, Sallie," I said still groggy. "Did we win or what?"

"It's pending. The arbitration board will decide when and where a voting will be held. Until then, it's out of our hands. We can still keep the picket line at a distance, but we can't prevent anyone from entering the plant. We'll have to work this more from the inside now. A few may get some personal visits...y' know what I mean?"

My hand went to my head as I felt the bandage. "Who pulled me outta this mess? You, Sallie?"

He only grinned and replied, "Let's go. Connie's waiting."

"Thanks," I said with my hand on his shoulder this time. "That's another one I owe you."

CHAPTER 9

▼

DARKER ASSIGNMENTS

Chapter Nine

"Tom, I missed you so much...I can't explain how I felt when I heard you were hurt. But I felt the pain just as if I was hurt too. I can't stay away from you."

Connie's hand touched my cheek.

"Tom, I need you. I want you."

She slipped into my arms and I held her close. Through her thin dress I felt the quivering tension coursing through her body as our lips met in a warm, tender kiss. As I glanced into her eyes they turned from a look of concern to one of passion. I kissed her again, hard on her lips, and as her mouth opened slowly, I felt the liquid fire of her tongue as it entered my mouth.

I counted the buttons on her blouse as I slowly opened them. She arched her back as I slipped her blouse off her shoulders and threw it away. She lay back on the bed with her eyes closed.

I reached around her body and unlocked the catch of her bra as she breathed deeply. She brought her arms around my neck and pulled me to her. I kissed her again and again, lips, flesh, always touching her smooth skin. Her body moved and trembled with the caress of my hands.

I felt her hands relax on my neck as they started to slide along my flesh tingling with excitement. Her legs locked around me as she began to scream in my ear. Deafening, we joined together into the softness of the bed over and over again, until we were exhausted.

After a long while, I raised my head and stole a look at her. She lay there on the bed looking happy and contented. Though her eyes were closed, she must have felt my penetrating gaze because she opened hers slowly, and smiled at me.

"Tom, I'm glad I'm here. You know that...I have never felt like this before. You make me feel such desire. I never knew I possessed such feelings. I love you, truly, I do."

She nestled against me and I realized she really had fallen in love with me.

"Tom, share my world...I need you so much. You make me feel so happy, so alive. I want to stay here with you, live with you, take care of you...be waiting for you when you come home."

I gently extricated myself from her warmth and touch. I had to tell her. It wouldn't work. I wasn't in love with her and I didn't intend to fall in love either. How did she sense this instinctively?

"You don't feel the same way, do you? You want to let me down gently. I don't care. I'll be content to be near you. That's all I ask. Don't you see, you'll feel as if you were coming home, a real home, because someone will be waiting…someone who loves and needs you, and that's me, Tom. That's just the way I feel. Please let me stay with you."

"Connie, that's not it. I'm lonely too and it would be wonderful to have you here, but it's not gonna work. There are too many obstacles. Our work, for instance. I don't like the idea of you working for the union."

"But, honey, you do the same type of work. If it's not wrong for you, why is it wrong for me? It's part of my life. It's in my blood, just like it's in your blood. Why can't we share this together? It seems like the almost perfect idea."

"Connie, I'm a man. I believe a man does a man's work and it's tough enough when a woman gets involved in the union. Look at what happened at Butler. I wouldn't want you involved in another mess like that. Suppose something serious had happened? I would never forgive myself."

"Look, let's just leave it as is. Let's live from day to day and take whatever comes. Whatever happens, happens…"

She leaned over me and kissed me, again. "You won't be sorry, I promise you that…so, it's settled?…I'm moving in?"

After a long pause, I agreed.

"Alright, Connie…"

I wasn't, sorry, ever. It was wonderful having her there. And she was right, I looked forward to coming home. I even found myself spending more and more time there. My loneliness was replaced with such amazing happiness and contentment. Perhaps, I was in love, after all.

Connie went about her work, but we never worked together. Somehow John found out about our arrangement…they have eyes and ears everywhere, these union bosses. But, John must have approved because he kept her working separately on the smaller strikes we were handling, and made sure that I wasn't distracted by her being near me wherever I worked.

"Tom," John said to me as I sat in his office.

"I have a special job for you. There's a shop which we're trying to organize. The majority of the workers were ready to sign, but then someone threw a monkey wrench into the machinery. The son of a bitch has gotten to the workers just enough to stop us from taking over.

"Our work has been stalled long enough. It's about time we just eliminated this bastard. This is where I need you. An accident. Arrange a good
one for him and silence him, for awhile. You don't have to kill him...Just
silence him for a good while!

"However, this assignment is risky. We can't afford to become involved.
If you get pinched, you're on your own. We will pay you...royally."

He took out a thick envelope and handed it to me.

"Count it. I hope you can see our point. Well, that's it. It's now up to
you. Do you want it or not?'

"Of course, I want it," I almost shouted back. "Do you think I joined this
union and have been with you for so long if I only wanted a job with no
danger or risk? Hell, no. And, don't you worry about me getting pinched. I
have no intentions of that."

"Good. I knew you would accept this job, but I had to lay it on the line,
and make sure it was your own personal decision. You'll work with Sal. He'll
give you all the details. He's downstairs waiting for you. Good luck!"

Sallie waited in the car as I went upstairs to pack.

"Connie, I have to go away. Maybe a week or so. Some unfinished business. There's money in the drawer in case you need it."

She didn't question me and helped me pack. As we made small talk it
became evident she was worried. Occasionally, I glanced her way and she
would force a smile, but I knew she was camouflaging her anxiety.

When we finished packing, I took out my hidden thirty-two, checked to
see if it was loaded, and slipped it in my pocket.

Connie looked at me and gasped, "Honey, no, no guns...what the hell are
you doing? What kind of job is this?"

"Connie, I don't need hysterics. I told you in the beginning that this
arrangement of ours wouldn't work. Not if our work interferes with our private lives. This is not your business. Please don't spoil things. I like, very
much, our being together, but I have a job to do. No one's gonna stop me
from going through with this, not even you."

"I'm not trying to stop you, honey. It's just that I'm worried. I worry all
the time but this time is different. I never saw you take a gun with you
before...please honey...don't go...maybe you should turn down this assignment...for me...please..."

I took her in my arms and gently kissed her.

"Connie, I can take care of myself. Don't worry. I'll be back soon. Nothing is gonna happen...stop being so tragic...I love you. I would never jeopardize that."

"I know, Tom...I love you too...just be careful...I love you so."

Connie brushed away a tear and kissed me softly...for a long time...I can still remember her moistened eyelashes as she slipped both her sadness and love to my cheek.

Sallie had the address where our man lived. We were fortunate to find a room to rent across the street from him, and took turns keeping watch and sleeping. We finally spotted him two days after our arrival. Looking out the window I saw a small man, about thirty-five or forty years old, five feet six inches tall, who couldn't have weighed more than a hundred and forty-five pounds.

"Why is it, Sallie, that these little guys make the most noise?"

"I don't know, Tom, but after this I'm betting he doesn't make much noise...let's see what he's gonna do."

We followed him up the street staying almost a block behind him. He entered a restaurant and we walked in a few moments later. Sallie and I sat at the counter while our man sat in the formal dining area ordering a full course meal. When he finished and paid his check, we timed finishing too, just a little behind him. We again, continued following him. He walked around aimlessly for awhile and then went home.

"Apparently, he hasn't a car. That makes it a little difficult," Sallie commented.

"I'll say. A car accident would have been easier to arrange. Or we could have just waited inside his car for him and grabbed him."

"Well, it's just gonna make it a little tougher. We'll have to figure some other fuckin' way to get to him."

"Do you want to kidnap him? Work him over and dump him somewhere?"

"We'd have to scout the area for some outta the way place to take him. I don't know."

"Well, let's just keep him under surveillance and see where he goes regularly...where he might be vulnerable..."

We kept him continuously in our sight, but we couldn't get anywhere near him. He was definitely a man with a constant, daily routine which should have made it easier. But it didn't. We just couldn't snatch him off the street in broad daylight. He avoided isolated places and rarely went out past dark, and tended to stick to places that knew him.

"Look, Sallie. We aren't getting anywhere this way. It's been a week and we aren't closer to him then when we first came here. Somethin' has to be done, and I think I know what it is."

"Every night since we started watching him, he comes home...then, he goes out to eat; then, he takes a short walk, right? Now each night at approximately eight he gets home, and once home, he stays put. He never leaves his apartment again until he's ready to go back to work in the morning.

"Here's what I was thinking. What if we get into his apartment and wait for him to come home? He lives on the first floor so it shouldn't be too hard to get in. We can do the job then and there. Whattaya think?"

"Sounds good, Tom. Beats sitting around here doing nothing. But when do you want to do it?"

"I figure the sooner, the better. Tomorrow night should be a good time as any."

"Should we break in when he's home, or break in while he's out eating?"

"I'd like to get in while he's eating, because he takes his usual walk. Then he can walk into us. That way no one will notice he's missing from work until the next day. And we'll be long gone."

Sallie told our temporary landlady that we were checking out. It was rented by the week, so the timing was perfect. We loaded the bags in the car and drove off to give the impression that we were really leaving town. Then we drove around for a while to kill time before circling back to town.

After parking a few blocks away from his apartment, we looked for the rear entrance to the building and found it was unlocked. No one saw us enter. When we got to his doorway, Sallie took out a ring of keys and picks. One, two, three, the lock clicked and the door opened. I gave one quick glance down the hall to make sure it was vacant, and in we slipped.

The lights were out. Our man was busy eating at the moment at a restaurant.

"Don't put on any lights." We waited for a minute or so until our eyes became accustomed to the darkness. "Go take the light bulbs out. When he comes home, I don't want him turning on any lights. We can take him by surprise then."

I could make out a kitchenette and a small bedroom. A lounge chair was near the bed. I made myself comfortable there while Sallie looked out the window. And, we waited.

It was only about two hours of a wait, but it seemed like a whole day. Sallie was becoming impatient and restless. He was eager for action and the waiting was making him edgy. Finally, just around eight o'clock, our vigil paid off.

We heard a key in the door. I slipped off the chair and walked quietly behind the door. Sallie crept to the other side.

The door opened and a slight ray of light slipped into the room. Our man went to close the door as his hand started flipping the light switch. Nothing. I kicked the door close and whirled into action. I grabbed his coat collar and with one hand pulled him towards me. The other hand smashed his shocked face.

I hit him a few more times.

"Stay away from the fuckin' shop. Leave town if you know what's good for you. And, you're not fuckin' walking anywhere tomorrow," Sallie muttered in a disguised, low voice.

I hit him again and drove my fist deep into his stomach. He grunted as he doubled over.

"This is what you get when you fuckin' fight our union. Stay out, get it?" I whispered to him as Sallie pulled him up by his collar and slammed his knee into his jaw. He collapsed and was unconscious.

I went over to the sink and threw a pail of water on him. He mumbled and moaned but could hardly get up.

"Remember, stay out. Stay away from the shop and the workers, or we'll kill you next time."

"Here's something to remind you."

Sallie went for his jaw. The man twisted somehow and got spun around into my heavy fist. The crunching of his bones echoed through the room and his jaw broke.

"That's enough," I said, grabbing Sallie by the arm. "We don't wanna kill him. Let's get the hell outta here just in case someone heard and called the cops."

As we left the building, sirens screamed out in the distance, and the cops pulled up...

CHAPTER 10

▼

INVISIBLE WOUND

Chapter Ten

"That was a tight call, Tom…yeah…What'd they think? We were gonna stick around"?

We were driving slowly now, passing a bottle between the two of us.

"Do you think it'll make the papers, Sal?"

"Probably. Who do'y think called the cops?"

"Someone with thin walls and an even thinner brain. Should mind their own fuckin' business…I don't like it, Sallie. I was sloppy. I should've jumped him and dragged him somewhere else. Suppose they go around and start asking questions? Suppose they find out about two strangers who mysteriously disappear just before this guy was half beaten to death? We should've gone and stayed somewhere else for a few days. Then doubled back to do the job."

"Well, no place like home Tom," Sallie said as we pulled up to my apartment. "I'm gonna lose the car's tags. We're owed a favor down at Harry's. He can repaint the car. See you around, okay?"

"Yeah. We should split up for a while. Just in case. If you get pinched, even for just questioning, get in touch with Vinnie or John. They'll get in touch with me so I can lie low. I'll do the same for you…let's meet up in about a month after this blows over."

"Sounds good. You take care of Connie up there."

"You know I will," I said. "Maybe we'll take a brief vacation."

I was already slightly drunk by the time I walked in on Connie. I could see she was overjoyed and very relieved to see me in one piece and home at last.

"Hey, Connie!"

"Hi, honey! I sure did miss you!"

"Can you get me the bottle of Jack Daniels?"

"Here's the bottle and the glasses, I'll pour the drinks…what did you do to your hands, my God. You're bleeding."

"It's nothing, but here I've ruined your tablecloth."

Without a word, Connie got out a basin of water and bandages and began to clean and dress my knuckles. I emptied my glass as fast as I could fill it.

"Lousy stinking mess," I murmured.

"Why do you do it, Tom?"

"Connie, not now. All I wanna do is get good and drunk."

"Do you want something to eat?" She barely got the words out and started to sob.

"Connie. Stop it. It was no big deal."

"Honey, please, I don't like to see you like this. Every time you go out on an assignment, it seems it takes something out of you. And, when it does, it's as if a part of me goes too. Don't you understand? You're good, Tom. Why don't we just leave the union? Get out of this business. It makes you sick after awhile, doesn't it? We could go somewhere, start over."

"Oh, Connie. You know you love your union work. You said so yourself. You're helping people. People who have nothing, no rights, no benefits, no one to fight for them."

"But, Tom. Every time they send you out you don't come home the same man anymore. I know it tears you apart. You can't fool me. You try to be hard as nails but deep down you have a heart of gold...I would know. You wear an invisible coat of armor trying to be rough and tough but your steel surface is only skin deep."

"Connie, you are a jewel. But I'm not a quitter. And I'm not a coward. I'm not going to quit just because the going gets rough. I told you before, I'll do my job but I don't have to like it. It's strictly business."

"Oh, please just go to John and tell him you want out. I know he'll release you from all obligations. He likes you. He'll do what's best for you.

"We could get married, Tom. You could have a family. We could even get your kids and raise them ourselves."

"I'm not getting married, Connie. Don't even mention it. It has nothing to do with you. I like what we have here, between the two of us, very much, but we're not tying the knot. And I can't take care of my kids. They're better off where they are. I still love my wife, you know. I can't bear the thought of replacing her."

"You're just drunk...you'll get over her death."

"NO!" I shouted. "Never...let's talk about somethin' else."

I was getting more drunk now. That's what I wanted, wasn't it? Just to forget for a little while, that's all. I could still hear that guy's wincing moan and the sound of his jaw cracking...I shook my head from side to side trying to get rid of the picture going off in my mind.

"I missed you so, honey," Connie cuddled up to me and sat on my lap, playing with my hair. Those eyes again. What a temptress. I was lucky here too, and before you could spell my full name we were in bed again together.

A whole week without her was somewhat unbearable. All I had to do was touch her lips and breasts, and the soft skin between her thighs, and you couldn't tear me away. This went on for hours and hours. Just her twisted around me and locked together. In the morning, she looked like the angel of fire and passion. All this desire and love and it all belonged to me.

"Tom, it was so lonely without you," Connie raised herself on her elbows and looked so deep into my eyes I was almost hypnotized by her stare.

"I went to church a few times this week. It seemed to inspire me. I can't explain it but it seems to have incited this overwhelming feeling of love. A kind of determination to better my life, our life together. We should go there one of these days, hon. Do you think we could?"

I felt as if I was just thrown a fly ball. I burst into an uproarious laughter that filled the room.

"Me, go to church? Is something wrong with you, Connie? You must be kidding. You know I think religion is a farce."

"Don't talk that way, honey. You can't be serious."

"I am Connie. Very serious."

"Why do you feel this way?"

"I never got the answer I was looking for. What's to believe in?"

"What are you talking about, Tom? What answer? To what question?"

I looked at her through bleary eyes and saw two of her, both very beautiful.

"Connie, in my home town I found so much happiness once. I married a wonderful woman who I loved very deeply. She bore me three sons, I had a beautiful marriage and family, my own business, and I was prosperous. Then one day, practically overnight, everything stopped. My wife died, and I cried until there were no more tears. Then I drank because I could no longer face life without her. I asked God, why? Why did I have to lose her and everything that was good? I never got an answer."

"Oh, Tom. Please don't think this way."

"Connie. I remember there was a tavern in my home town, somewhat known in certain circles as a whorehouse. Those God damn girls there, hell, they would dance with anyone who would buy them a drink. But they were nothing but whore's. I'd down a few drinks and watch them. But drinking only made me see my one and only, my beloved Mary, who I had lost...as I lost myself too, in a bottle...

"Why, I asked myself, would God take so wonderful a woman, someone who in her entire life had never harmed a soul? How could he take her from her adoring husband and the lives of her three devoted children? And there, across the way from me, they sat. The slut's and whore's, laughing and dancing and whoring, and those he keeps alive and enjoying life.

"No one can tell me that an all loving and all powerful, higher being could allow that. I have seen little babies taken from their mothers' arms, while others with nothing but loneliness, suffering and nothing to look forward to, live to the ripe old ages of seventy and eighty or more..."

"Oh, Tom, Tom...if we were as smart as God, himself, we would have no need of Him. If you don't find an answer, I know He can give you peace of mind. I'm not the authority, and I know I'm not living the way He would want me to, but I do know that He is always there, waiting to take my hand when I need Him...He's always there waiting with open arms for anyone who needs HIM, and that includes you, Tom."

"I don't need anyone Connie...I live in my own world. I live it hard and die harder, and as far as I'm concerned, that's all there is."

I saw the pained expression on her face. "I'm sorry." I said.

"You do care, don't you honey? You know, I do, and each day it grows stronger, this love in my heart for you, Tom."

"Of course, I do, Connie. It's just hard sometimes. I just wanted you to know why...I'm so tired..."

"I love you, Tom. You go to sleep. You should stay in after this last job. Watch those knuckles, and sleep...I have to get going..."

She leaned over me and kissed me, then headed out the room to get dressed for work.

The ringing of the phone woke me. I tried to get out of bed but the pounding in my head only knocked me out cold again. I was very hung over. It rang again, and I finally limped over to the phone.

"Whoever's calling, go away! And leave me the hell alone!" I yelled into the receiver and slammed it down.

On the kitchen table I saw a letter.

Honey,

I have to go to work. You fell asleep and were sleeping so soundly I hated to wake you. There's some coffee on the stove. You better drink it black.

You're going to have a real headache when you wake up. I'll give you a call later.

All my love,
Connie

I smiled to myself. The phone was ringing again and I picked it up.
"Hello?"
"Tom. This is Sallie. You have to get to the hospital real quick. Did you hear me? It's Connie!"
"What?"
"Just get here fast. You're wasting time. She got hit...she doesn't have long."
The phone line went dead. Connie, I said to myself. Connie, what's the matter, what the hell happened? I yelled into the empty receiver.
I dressed fast and drove like a mad man. There was a cold glove near my heart. I could not shake it. At the hospital, Sallie was waiting in the emergency ward.
"Room 505, Tom. She's asking for you, hurry. There isn't much time."
I vaguely saw the doctor and the Priest as I rushed past them into her room. My eyes fell on Connie, lying there on the bed so still and pale, with blood stained bandages all over her. She tried a weak smile and then her whole face convulsed with pain.
I felt powerless to help her. I kissed her on the cheek and tried a small joke, but it barely left my throat. All I could see now instead of fire and love, was death in her eyes, glassy and distant.
Her eyes, I will never forget her eyes. Such sadness when she looked at me as one tear after another slipped down her beautiful face.
"Hold me honey," she whispered weakly. "I'm afraid."
I took hold of her hand and tried to hold her tightly in my arms but she was in too much pain to be touched. She clung to my neck and I held her like fragile china.
"Don't say that, Connie. There's nothing to fear. Nothing is going to happen to you...I won't let it."
"Tom," she whispered. "I love you so."
"Don't talk. I love you too. You need your strength."

I kissed her again. For just a flash of a second, her eyes almost looked like they used too, radiating, happy. I felt her body go limp as her arms slipped from around my neck.

"No, Connie!" I yelled, shaking her by the shoulders. I felt someone trying to pull me from her but I held onto her tightly. They had to tear me away. Don't die on me...please, honey, don't die on me...I lost her...again and again, I always lose in the end...not again, God...the second woman I ever really loved...the only one who ever meant anything to me after my wife died...why God, why?

I staggered from her room. I saw no one and passed by everything in a daze. I don't even remember how I got home. Everywhere I turned I could see her. She was in the kitchen cooking, in the bedroom dressing, lying there near my pillow. I saw ghosts. Every time I turned I saw her.

I was touching the fabric of one of her dresses when I heard Sallie speak.

"Tom, get hold of yourself damn it, I don't want to see you crack." That almost jolted and snapped me out of it. But, suddenly, I couldn't quite hear him. The room became cloudy, hallucinations appeared, then just cold dark. There was a long, silent pause in the room. I had been staring at her dress, for how long? An hour? Finally, I turned around and saw Sallie.

"How the hell did it happen? She told me she was on a quiet strike and it was almost over. What could've gone wrong?"

"We were on the line and everything was going along smoothly. Then this crazy bastard drove his car right into the line...I pushed people out of the way, but I was too late.

"The force of the car had smashed her against the wall and crushed her. She was so badly injured, the doctor didn't think she would make it to the hospital. I think she held on only so she could see you again.

"I'm sorry, Tom. I know you loved each other very much. Is there anything I can do for you?"

"No, no. We were very happy, the time we spent together. The love she had for me. So much. I doubt I ever returned it in full. But she didn't ask for anything more. She just seemed happy and contented just being with me."

"She was happy with you, Tom. When I first met Connie, she seemed to drift from day to day, just working for the union. It became her whole life. Then you two met, and she changed completely. Life seemed to become more precious to her. She never wanted to lose a single minute of time that she could be with you."

As Sallie talked, I realized how much Connie meant to me. She wanted nothing more than to make me happy. All she asked in return was for us to stay together. I wanted to hold her one more time. Tell her how much I really cared. I wanted her back so desperately. I wanted to see her just one more time, laughing and talking with that beautiful fire in her eyes. To hold her again in my arms. Just one more time. But it was too late. She was gone.

"I want that son of a bitch" I suddenly shouted. "I want him bad, real bad...we never did find Mike's murderer, but this time...I swear it...if it's the last thing I do. I'll find the bastard and I'll...no matter what I do to him..."

I wanted to kill.

"Tom, we all want to avenge Connie's death. We will. Not you. You'd be working in a blind rage. You'd just end up getting hurt. You'd throw all caution to the wind and fuck up. We do know who killed her. But you have to cool off first. The police have him anyway, right now."

I didn't need a cooling off period. I could do what had to be done, for Connie, but I knew he was right at the same time.

"Cool off first, Tom. Later, when you can think and plan a little more clearly, we'll talk about this. I'll let you get rid of the bastard. But you have to snap out of this first."

"Alright, Sallie. I'll take some time off. Can you take care of the funeral arrangements? Here's some money. She didn't have any family. I just can't stand around and watch her get lowered into the ground."

"I'll take care of everything Tom."

I sat in my apartment for years it seemed. Death was such a final thing. You couldn't change it. You couldn't cure it. I couldn't even bring myself to go through her belongings. I got rid of her cat. I just opened the window and let it out.

In the beginning, all I could remember was Connie as I reeled from bar to bar. It was better this way. All the sharp edges became softer. Then I could start forgetting. What did I care? I didn't. It was as if someone had ripped me open and tore me up inside. But these were invisible wounds...they hurt even more...never healed. No, I don't think I ever did...heal.

CHAPTER 11

▼

AN EYE FOR AN EYE

Chapter Eleven

"Alright, get up." I heard a voice from somewhere. I lifted my head and it felt like it weighed a ton. My bleary, bloodshot eyes glanced around the room. Miraculously it was my own place I had finally landed in. The voice was Sallie's.

"Hi," I mumbled.

"Did you have enough booze, Tom? Or do you want to go for some more?..."

"NO...I guess I have just about had it. I'm finished. I don't want anymore."

"Are you ready to go to work?"

I stood up. My clothes were clearly crumpled, and the food and coffee in the kitchen was cold and old.

"I need to shower. Get some breakfast. Whattaya got?"

"You wanted the information on who killed Connie. Y' know, it may not have been a cold blooded and deliberate murder."

"You sure?"

"Well, even in our line of work, Tom, accidents can happen. There are always risks. The guy was arrested, but got off. They believed his story that his foot slipped on the accelerator causing the car to burst ahead."

"You believe that? Give me a fuckin' break."

"He could have been distracted by the picket line. He could have pretended to be distracted. Hard to say. But John wants it clear to everyone that we protect our own. The book states an eye for an eye. How Connie died was a vile thing.

"John picked you for the job, not because of your relations with Connie, but because we both feel you're the best man for the job. Understand, Tom, you're on an assignment, not an act of revenge...with that in mind, here's John's instructions. Do it the right way. Make the right statement. Don't do anything stupid and don't get pinched."

"Here's John's private phone number. Call him when you're finished from a pay phone. Guess y' know now what that black phone is used for."

Sallie handed Tom an envelope, and left quickly. Inside was cash, as usual, and a name and street address:

Raymond Gulino
119 95th Street

I waited until night fall, then set out with my trusted war knife and gun in hand. As I drove my car, the extreme hatred I had for this man, who had taken everything from me, burned inside. It burned real bad. They do say revenge is a sweet medicine.

I didn't give a shit about Sallie and John's instructions. Be cool, objective, this is not a job about revenge. Oh really? I know why they fuckin' picked me. They knew I would take care of this guy. So they manipulated my hate. Or did I manipulate them for the guy's name and address, since I wanted to be the killer? The world gets a little complicated, doesn't it?

I parked my car a short distance from his house and waited. I could afford to be patient. Four hours later, still nothing. I was ready to leave, when a pair of headlights flashed along the deserted street. It turned into his driveway and it was my man.

I flew across the street like a silent hawk. He was just turning his ignition key off when I shoved my forty-five through the car window and aimed straight at his brain. I thought I would blast him right on the spot. For some reason I hesitated. I wanted him to know why first…wanted him to crawl first in fear.

"Ray," I said. "Ray Gulino?"

He looked real scared. I don't think he could talk at first. Everything was choked behind his tongue and he broke out in a heavy sweat. Finally, he mumbled, "I'll fuckin' give you anything you want. Money? What? Anything…"

Imagine. He thought he could buy his way out of this one.

"Get outta the fuckin' car, you bastard!"

I opened the car door, reached in and grabbed him by the collar yanking him into the street. You little piece of shit, I thought. I shoved my forty-five into his ribs and pushed him towards my car.

"What…" he started to say again.

"Shut up, you son of a bitch and move it, or I'll drop you right here. Now get in this car. You're going to take a little drive. The keys are in the ignition, and I'm gonna sit right next to you and so is this little gun."

I shoved him in through the passenger side watching his legs turn to putty beneath him.

"Head for the tunnel, and don't talk. Don't attract anyone's attention and you may just get out of this alive."

I hated his guts. I hated his blood. I almost wanted him to try to warn someone so I'd have an excuse to blast him right here. "Yeah, just open your mouth. I have nothing to lose. I don't care what happens to me."

He nodded and didn't say a word. In fact, he peed his pants as we drove towards the tunnel. I took us out to the meadows. When we got to the spot I wanted, I told him to stop the car. It was totally isolated and almost pitch black No one could ever help him. I barked at him, "GET THE FUCK OUT!"

I put the gun to his head and he fell to his knees. Grabbing my leg, he started to cry like a baby and beg. I almost pulled the trigger. You want to be a murderer, Tom? This is going to bring Connie back? Maybe the union's unwritten law would be better. Give him something to remember for the rest of his life. We decide what the justice is for certain acts. An eye for an eye.

I raised my hand and hit him across the head with the gun. His body sank heavily to the ground, blood gushing from the head wound. He passed out. I rolled him over on his back and sat astride his chest. From my pocket I pulled out my knife.

As he started to rouse, I brought the knife near his face. As he opened his eyes, I flicked the switch...the blade snapped out in all its brilliance, gleaming in the intermittent moonlight, and the fear grew in his eyes.

I placed the point of the blade against his throat.

"Remember the woman you supposedly accidentally killed last week?...At the picket line?"

A whimpering sound squeezed out from the back of his throat. I didn't let him talk. Just so that he knew why this was going to happen to him. I grabbed the front of his shirt, ripped the cloth, and slashed his chest.

A scream of pain struck the night. I hit him and knocked him out. I looked at his face with disgust. The blade had made a gash from his right shoulder down to the left side of his belt.

"That's for Connie..." I whispered.

He started to regain consciousness in a few minutes, and I just slashed again, this time completing an X on his body. He screamed once more and passed out again.

"That's for Mike..."

I wasn't finished. He was going to show his scars for life. I grabbed him savagely by the hair and twisted his face to the side. The knife reached out again like it had a mind of its own and cut through his right cheek.

"That's for Connie, again."

I turned his face around and cut open the left side now.

"And, that's for me."

I knew this guy would never be the same person. I was covered in blood but it meant nothing to me. He was an ugly mess, but I felt strangely satisfied, and was glad he would always know why he was carrying those scars. I left him there in the swamps. Let him find his own way out, tortured, sick son of a bitch.

I had to clean myself up first. I always had a spare set of clothes in the car. It was easy to find just the right dim lit motel and pry open a door to use the bathroom and shower. Then I got rid of the bloody clothes, drove off, and stopped at a pay phone. I gave John a call.

"Hello?"

"Hi. It's done. Everything went smoothly. I'll tell you the details later...good night."

Two days later, I was called in to see John.

"It made the papers."

"Yeah, I thought it would."

"You didn't waste him, huh?"

"Death would've been too easy a sentence for him. I decided to give him something to remember for life...maybe, I'll visit him again sometime...give him something else to remember...the son of a bitch."

"Good!..You got this outta your system and we took care of business, properly...I have some good news for you, Tom. The boss upstairs decided to open the books and grant me a request."

"A request, John?"

"Yeah, Tom. He's opening the books and making you a boss! You're going down to Florida to have a crew, your OWN crew now. There's been a big problem down there for some time.

"No new shops have been signed up in about a year. Jack Gussona...he's the man you'll be replacing. The big boss wants you down there. See what you can do for him, okay?"

"I don't know what to say. Of course, I'll go."

"Tom, you've come a long way since you became a union member. I told you once I can spot a good union man a mile away and when I seen and heard you, I knew I had an ace in the hole. You're making a big leap here...I have no fear that you can handle the job, but a word of advice.

"You're now going to be giving orders, not taking them. Remember that. Don't take any shit on that one. And don't get in over your head. Don't get carried away. Always plan. Think first. Think clearly."

"I understand. Thank's John. I won't disappoint you."

"I know you won't. You already done more than I can ask, you're always there when I need you. I know that you'll do a good job down there. When do you think you can leave? It'll be good for you, in any event...take your mind off this Gulino fellow...and Connie...you could use a change."

"You're right, John...the sooner the better, but, maybe give me a week or so. You wanna take over my apartment for the time being? It's just a kitchen and a small bed room, furnished. Could come in handy. Someone always needs a place to stay. Sallie said so the first time he stayed over."

"Sounds good."

"I'll drop off the keys later. Yeah, let me get a few matters straightened out. I guess a week should do it."

I thought about Connie, the boys, the apartment...it was better this way...leave it all behind me, was getting excited about Florida. I forced a smile and some exuberance as John and I toasted the future, but my heart was still heavy. Time, I needed time and a change of pace. I needed to forget...good old John, thinks of everything doesn't he?

CHAPTER 12

▼

THE NEW BOSS

Chapter Twelve

Two gals, both pretty…one just a teenager practically, sat behind the counter and completely ignored me when I walked into the office. It was a small, bare office with a haphazard arrangement of two empty desks, filing cabinets, and a few chairs.

"Is Mr. Gussona in?"

I received a blank, dumb stare from one of the girls. Perhaps they didn't hear me. I repeated.

"Tell Mr. Gussona that Mr. Furcco is here."

The older one wasn't that bad to look at. My eye involuntarily gave her the once over but I wasn't interested. I was her new boss. She snapped out of her trance and spoke rapidly as if to hide her embarrassment.

"Mr. Gussona is expecting you, Mr. Furcco. Just go through the open door."

"Thanks, hon."

On the other side of the door was a larger office filled with boxes and papers. Seated behind the desk was a small built man about forty-five years old, with grey around the temples of his head, hunched over a piece of paper in his hand, studying it intensely.

"Jack?" I inquired.

"Yeah, oh! You must be Tom. Glad to meet you."

He rose to shake my hand.

"They told me you were coming down soon. I have everything ready for you. You can take over whenever you want."

"No hurry, Jack. I want to look everything over first. Tell me what's goin' on? How many employees do we have?"

"We have sixteen employees…ten crew members and six in the office. Not much compared to your operation up North, I'm afraid."

"I see. And how are things goin' getting shops to sign up? New York seems to think that it's much too slow."

"Well, that's just it. We've been trying to organize these shops. They're fuckin' ripe for the picking because there's just so few unions down here to begin with. Not much competition for us. But the workers are transient. That's a hard bunch to work with. There just doesn't seem to be much union desire, or they are just plain divided. They want unions but they're afraid of losing their jobs. Or the foremen threatens to fire anyone if they even talk union or even strike. You know, that kind of shit."

"How many shops have you been able to sign up so far?"

"In the past two years since I've been down here, I've had the distinction of organizing five shops. But it was hard work and I'm fuckin' proud of that record. I'm telling you, this is a very hard sell down here. No one's interested."

"That's bullshit, Jack. How many shops are down here altogether? And, I mean in all lines of work."

"About two hundred."

"And, we've only got five signed? Why do the workers move around so much? Is that what you meant by transient? What is it about down here?"

"Sunshine, Tom. The great warm temps and sunshine. They flock down here in droves. Helps the employers out especially. With more employees than jobs, they can keep wages low, and if you mention a union, you can be easily replaced by another worker."

"That's the problem?"

"I've tried my best, Tom, especially with such a small crew. You have some new ideas."

"Yeah, Jack. I have a few. But I'd like to start out slowly. Always think before you act, I say. One thing though, I would like you to work with me. I know you were ordered back to New York. But that doesn't mean you have to go. I'd like to keep you as my right hand man."

"Hell, Tom. Yeah, I would like to stay on."

"I'm an union man, Jack, and the good of the union comes first. I feel you can help me out here. You are more familiar with the shops, y' know your crew, and y' know what's out there. Whattaya say?"

"Tom, if staying down here would help you and the union, I'm in. You'll see, your own family will like living down here. Mine does. The atmosphere is nice."

"I'm solo right now, Jack. Better that way. But I could use your help to find a nice place to live in."

"I already have a few places picked out. We can look at them today if you like."

"Good. Work with me and cooperate, and in a short time we'll show the New York Bosses we know how to organize shops. There's one other thing I want to bring up. Now that I'm your boss, I need you to always follow my orders, no matter what. It's very important."

"Not a problem, Tom."

"We'll have enough problems stopping us along the way. If there isn't any loyalty with my crew, our work will be in vain. I don't wanna have to fight you or anyone in my crew."

"What do you think Tom, I'm an half ass wise-guy? I'll fuckin' go along with any order you give me."

A few days later, I had my first union meeting with the new Florida crew. I stood in front of the union hall and looked at them. Jack introduced me as their new boss, but I got the feeling they already knew that...I had to get the ball rolling, so to speak, and get some energy and planning going.

"Listen, people, My name is Tom Furcco, just in from New York, and I am your new boss."

I paused. Nothing. Their faces were blank, no response.

"We've got to turn this situation around down here or New York is going to replace all of you. I'm the one they picked to reorganize this crew."

"I was asked to get rid of all of you. But, I said NO I said that you were all good for the industry. I have even asked Jack to stay on and continue working with me as my right hand man. So, let's start airing things out. I'm taking you all under my wing and I need you to work every single hour of the day practically with me. We're going to have a tough road ahead.

"Jack has had nothing but praise about you, and he knows you the best. He says you can follow orders without bitching, and without insolence. I trust his opinion. You are all in very good hands. I plan to have a personal meeting with each and everyone one of you so we'll be the tightest union labor organizers in the country!"

"That's right...IN THE COUNTRY. The union has sent me out in the field on some very tough assignments and each time I didn't fail them. Each time I produced more than either they or myself even expected. We're gonna do the same here."

"As I stated, already, I'm down here to organize shops. That's my primary purpose. How many shops do we have down here? One hundred, two hundred?...Whattaya want with five shops? Five shops in two years-and that's all you have to show for yourselves? Where's all the hard work?

"I'm gonna tell you what we're gonna do. We're going after every single one of those shops. Together, we'll try every shop regardless of how remote the chances are. You may think I set my sights too high, but one thing I know, I will not submit to defeat without a fight. This is gonna be a one way street, my one way street, and I expect you to go to the end of that street if I ask. "It's gonna be hard work, twenty-four hour shifts if necessary. We're gonna be on our feet all the time...handing out flyers, organizing meetings, walking picket lines, spreading the word that our union is the best in the business. We will go all out to accomplish our aims!

"And the pay off...the pay off is grand! Do you know how much we can bring in with two hundred shops? Do you? Do you know how many peoples lives you'll touch? The oppressed, the beaten up, the ones who have no one to fight for them, we can and will fight for them. Our union will save families. Husbands and sons won't have to work in sweat shops for dirt pay, won't have to drag himself to work when he's sick, don' have to work everyday of the year without a day off, or live in fear if they protest anything they'll get fired. Do you see how much you can do for these people? Do you understand why I was sent down here? Do you wanna make yourselves the greatest union organizers on the East Coast?"

This was the real day one for me. I was the new Boss.

Jack and I returned to my office to have a sit-down session.

"Jack, do you have any shops that have stalled, right now?"

"Splitezer's and Tilton's. I've been going after them for months but I can't seem to get any action going. In one shop, Tilton's, I've managed to sway ten men, but the rest won't budge."

"Why not, Jack?"

"It's a tough situation, Tom. They know they can take a risk about losing their jobs, but that's not their main concern. Most of 'em are married with families. They like their work, but they won't stay if they get opportunities for better paying jobs. So the big problem right now with them is money."

"So, you're saying that they know a union can fight for better wages. They must be afraid that if they bring a union in, and a strike happens, they won't be able to live with no money coming in. What about the other shop?"

"That shop. Most of the workers want a union. But the owner made it known very openly that no union is gonna run his shop. If he ever hears union talk mentioned in his shop he'll personally fire everyone responsible and another five arbitrary workers. He plays real tough. They're all afraid of losing their jobs now."

"He's tough, is he? Let's see how rough he wants to play. I've had this idea mapped in my head over the past few days. Now is a good time to bring it out. Here's what I want you to do. I want you to hire fifty of the toughest men, even a few women, that you can find. You can find them somewhere, even in other towns, and offer them seven dollars for every day they can work. I want 'em here tomorrow. I'll tell you what kind of work they'll be doing later. Also, I want the top two men you have for an assignment. Who can you give me?"

"That would be Jim Larosa and Buddy Sambino. They're the best in the field. Plenty of experience and they know the rules."

"Good. Here's a sample of the pamphlet I want made up. Get 'em printed quickly. Hell, yesterday was too late. Then have Jim and Buddy pass them out at Splitezer's. Tell 'em to talk to the workers. Tell the workers that we're having a meeting here tomorrow. I want Jim and Buddy to stress that it's very important for them to attend and it's for their benefit...

"Now, call Splitezer's right now and make an appointment for us to see him...a meeting with him is first on the agenda. Do you follow me so far?"

"Yeah, Tom. I do. But..."

"What? Tell me?"

"This isn't New York. You can't run this office the way you would there. I don't think Splitezer will budge."

"Jack. I said when I first met you, don't express doubt, don't question. Now get on that damn phone and make that fuckin' call."

"Alright Tom. I'm making it right now."

He returned a few minutes later looking forlorn.

"He doesn't want to see us. They practically told me to go shit in my hat."

"Okay. We'll do it another way. Do you have any information on him—full name, married, address, anything?"

"Yeah, His full name is Herman Splitezer. He's married with three kids. He lives in his own home in Hialeah. His business isn't booming—could be much better, but he isn't doing that bad."

"Let's go, Jack. We're paying a visit."

We drove to his little factory on sixty-fourth street and we parked the car. We walked around the side of the building until we came to the door sign that read "office." Inside, I spoke to the secretary seated there.

"I'm Mr. Furcco. This is Mr. Gussona. We like to see Mr. Splitezer."

"Do you have an appointment?"

"No, we don't. But we just talked on the phone. Tell him we didn't finish the conversation."

"I doubt he'll see you, but, very well, just a moment," she said in a quiet voice. "I'll see if he's busy."

She exited into a recessed office and closed the door. After a few moments, she returned.

"I'm sorry, but Mr. Splitezer is too busy to see anyone at the moment. You'll have to make an appointment for tomorrow."

I knew this was a run around. Tomorrow it'll be the same bullshit. Mr. Splitezer isn't in…I'm sorry Mr. Splitezer had to go to a meeting. Always, something like that.

"Tell Mr. Splitezer, that I wanna see him now and I won't take no for an answer. If he refuses to see me, tell him that I'll be forced to wait for him at his home along with his wife and children."

I spoke softly. I did not shout, but my intent was real and rung a bell with the secretary. She startled, moved back a pace, then practically ran back into Mr. Splitezer's office. After a few minutes, she returned and ushered us in.

The man behind the desk started to say something, but I stopped him cold.

"Mr. Splitezer, I presume. I think you know why we're here so I'll get right to the point. I hear your employees want a union in this shop, my union. I also hear you will fire anyone that talks union or demands a union. That's a very undemocratic way of doing business.

"Just hear me out. Since the majority of your men want our union to represent them, we will. We're here to discuss this with you. We can work out this whole thing in a congenial, intelligent manner or we can do it the hard way. It's up to you. Now here's what we propose and don't interrupt.

"Number one, we want to be the union in this shop. Number two, the men get a twenty-five cent an hour raise which will be paid in installments. Fifteen cents now, ten cents two months later. Number three, three days vacation. Number four, overtime pay after forty hours. Number five, a year's contract. We can iron out a lot of the smaller details after we start to draw up the papers. That's it. With your approval, of course."

"I will not…who the fuck are you…" he shouted.

"Hold it," I said patiently. "It won't be a one sided deal where you're giving everything and getting nothing in return. You have a small factory. Your profits are at a minimum. They could be much more. I intend to get that for you. I can get you contacts which you never dreamed of getting. If I start the ball rolling, your shop will be going full blast with more work than you can handle."

I paused, waiting for this to sink in. He didn't utter a word.

"So, that's the best way for you. This is how we'll handle things, if we have your cooperation. If not, then we'll be forced to do things the hard way. We will order a strike. Your men will all walk out. If you think you can just fire them and replace them, forget it. I have fifty men waiting for my orders. They will form a picket line so strong and powerful outside your shop, that no one will be able to get in. Your shop will be closed up tight."

"Once, again. You have a lot to gain by going with us. Just think of the extraordinary profit you can be making with us. If I were you, I'd think this matter over very carefully. I want your answer by tomorrow morning. Mr. Gussona will be in touch with you. Just let him know what your decision is. I guess we've covered everything. Good afternoon, Mr. Splitezer."

We left Mr. Splitezer dumbfounded and speechless. As we passed his secretary, she shied away from us as if we were gangsters or something. I thought that was kind of ironic. She probably expected bloodshed or gun play. I gave her a sinister look and said, "Don't worry sister. If your boss cooperates, everything will be okay."

CHAPTER 13

▼

OFF TO THE RACES

Chapter Thirteen

We were off to the races. In less than twenty-four hours, I had to organize a meeting, arrange for a picket line to wait on the sidelines if needed, secure contracts from New York, get pamphlets printed, draw up legal papers, contact Splitezer in the morning…

"Jack, we made a real impression on our Mr. Splitezer. I can tell. Give him a call first thing in the morning. I'll start the shit rolling about getting him some better contracts. You should call our attorney. We have one down here, don't we?"

"Yeah Tom."

"Tell the lawyer to draw up all the necessary papers. Tell him we get twelve and a half percent of the profits for each contract Splitezer accepts and fills. The workers, I intend to give them exactly what I said.

"One more thing, their dues have to be automatically deducted from their wages…three dollars and fifty cents a month with initiation fees of ten dollars. New member start up fees will be fifteen dollars. When the workers get their first raise, the dues go up to four dollars. We can have the initiation fees paid in installments…two dollars a week until the ten is paid."

"Don't the workers complain about the deductions and fees?"

"If you have it all done legally so that everything comes out of their pay before they receive it, you won't have any holdouts. And the workers don't complain once they see those new contracts coming in. They'll have all the overtime they want, plus the pay raises. It usually looks like a good deal to them.

"Now, you know, I know, it's bull-shit about having fifty men because I know you haven't had the time to find them yet. Here's how you should do it…when you meet with the crew…you said you had ten, right?…Assign each of them to find at least five strong, tough men a piece. Tell 'em we'll pay seven dollars a day. All they have to do is be on a picket line. Tell 'em we'll let 'em know if we need them tomorrow after you talk to Mr. Splitezer in the morning.

"Also, you need to get the pamphlets printed. Who were the top two men again? Jim and Buddy?"

"Yeah Tom, Jim and Buddy."

"You go over with them what they're supposed to do at the shop tomorrow: talk union, give out the flyers, announce our meeting…what's a good time to have the meeting, Jack?"

"Say about Noon, the shop's lunch hour?"

"That sounds good. Make sure that Jim and Buddy reinforce that the meeting is for the workers, their benefit. If they want pay raises and better conditions without the fear of being fired, then we can help...our union can help...especially since good paying jobs are scarce down here. Can the girls fix up a nice platter for the meeting?"

"Yeah, Tom, I'll tell them to take care of that."

"Good. Have Buddy and Jim invite the workers to free lunch then, not just a meeting. Refreshments, sandwiches and desert, something like that..."

"Tom, if Mr. Splitezer doesn't join, we're gonna have a damn fight on our hands."

"We have to consider that possibility. You'll have to talk to the workers at the meeting tomorrow and get them to sign cards. That'll help us in case we have trouble with the cops. You have any of them with us? You know what I mean?"

"The captain gets paid regularly. They usually look the other way."

"Good. Now, here we are, the office. Do you have everything straight, Jack? I'm counting on you."

"I'll be fine. Where will you be in case I need to reach you?"

"I wanna look over this town...visit a few places, so I won't be back at the office for the rest of the day. You can reach me at home late. I'll be in the office tomorrow, about mid-morning hope you'll have good news for me on the Splitezer call."

For the rest of the day and early the next day, I cruised around Miami and Hialeah. I toured the big, big factories. I needed to see what was around, the size, the numbers employed, the products, and the suppliers. I stopped off at a few offices, bull-shit-ed with the foremen and secretaries, pretended I was new in town, looking for work.

About ten AM the following day, I walked into the office. From the smiles on the girls' faces, I knew that Splitezer had signed. Jack was grinning from ear to ear.

"Damn it, Tom! I tried to get that son of a bitch for the past six months and got nowhere. You come along and do it in three days."

"I told you. They sent you the best, me! I figured he would come with us. There are two things in life that'll make a man's head turn...fear and money...did you get in touch with the lawyers?"

"We work quickly down here, when we need to. I gave them the amounts you wanted made legal, and they prepared a draft early this morning. The papers are sitting on your desk right now."

"Did New York call?"

"Tom, something came over the wire, I think from them," he said placing it in front of me. I opened the envelope. Inside, four different work order contracts.

"Jack, these are the contracts I told your about. Splitezer and the workers will be very happy. We're giving 'em what they want…this is great, Jack. I'm glad everyone's happy and contented. It'll make our work easier when we start working on the other shops. We'll have something to show 'em now besides promises. How does the crew feel today? They know?"

"I think they were probably a little leery when they first met you. But now that Splitezer has signed up, they're ready to follow orders. I know 'em. They really are enthused about working now."

"Okay. I'm gonna let you, Jim and Buddy run the meeting today. Just go with the usual bullshit, get the cards signed, the flyers out, make sure everyone has a good meal. Start with the best news, your boss has agreed to let our union represent you, and he has four, brand new contracts to show for it. Meet up with me later? I have a few things to discuss with you."

"How about the Mermaid's Bar and Grill, Tom?"

"Okay, I know where it is. About four PM?"

I walked into the cocktail lounge, sat down at the bar, and ordered my usual, Jack Daniels. Jack showed up shortly and we moved to a booth.

"The meeting went fine, Tom. You're right. Everyone seems happy. Very smooth. You know, I'm so glad they sent you down here."

"Thanks. But you're doing a lot here too. Couldn't have pulled it off without you."

"Thanks, Tom. That means a lot to me."

"I been pretty busy yesterday and today. I went looking at a few shops. I liked what I seen. I located six shops which look very good to me, each with about hundred employees or more. These are the kind of shops we need."

"Whattaya wanna do with 'em?"

"Y' know, from the union's point of view, we'll fare very well if we organize a big shop. New York will like that…like that very much…

"You see, a shop with a hundred workers, when organized the right way, brings in about four dollars a head. That's four hundred a month. The initiation fees add another twenty-five hundred dollars. Later we can throw in assessment charges at them for almost anything we can think of.

"Then there are the contracts which we get for them. That runs anywhere from twelve to forty percent for every contract we supply them with. In the course of a year, a shop can bring in from ten to thirty thousand dollars. And that goes on indefinitely, just like repeat business.

"I see it this way, Jack. The New York Bosses have placed me here to sign shops, and as long as there's a steady, climb uphill, they'll be more than pleased. The owner of the plant benefits because we're handing him extra contracts. I won't say he can't do this on his own, but we have bigger and faster connections. We can save him time, effort, and money.

"And the majority of the workers will be satisfied. They get steady work, sufficient overtime…"

"And, raises, vacations, and someone to back them when they have a beef. You're right, Tom. When the boss wanted to fire someone he did…just like that," Jack said snapping his fingers.

"Now it will be altogether different and both parties know that."

"So that's the way it is. The owner gets rich…the workers' working conditions improve. I sincerely feel that the money we receive for these services is well worth it."

"You know, Tom, your outlook on this whole business is right on the mark. Couldn't agree with you more. About those other, bigger shops…when do you want to start working them?"

"I would like to organize them all at once if I could."

"Don't you think that would be a big order, Tom?"

"No, I don't think so. There'll be complications and it may turn out to be a long and touchy grind. I'll have to think more on it. But this is what I want you to do now. I want you to send a man into each of the shops I picked out. Here are the shops' names, I wrote them down for you.

"Now, Jack, regardless of what position or salary is offered to our crew, I want 'em to accept it. Say they're new in town. Once they're in, I want 'em to circulate news, good news about our union…whenever they have idle conversations with other workers. We have to plant the seeds to make those workers aware that a union, a great union, is around and wants admittance into their shop."

"Okay!"

"Maybe, in a day or two, once you have picked out the six men to send out, we can have another meeting. I'll go over everything with 'em, and we can work out some details about how to spread the word. Later, if one of 'em can get his hands on other information, say worker names, addresses, we can use that information also. But, let's take this one step at a time."

"Hey, Tom...we're celebrating my son's birthday later tonight...a little party. My wife, cooks up a storm. Wanna join us?"

"Nah...that's alright, Jack. Maybe some other time. I feel a little restless right now. Always do, after signing up a shop. I think I'll take in some of the night spots in town tonight...blow off a little steam..."

Jack excused himself. I decided to try to relax a little, have a few more drinks. Planning, planning...everything went racing through my brain... yes, I needed to unwind a bit...that's right, Jack, you go home yourself and have a good time. I'll stay behind, and wonder a bit about mine, a good time, I mean...that's what I need.

CHAPTER 14

▼

THE NEXT ROUND-GEARING UP

Chapter Fourteen

I went to the bar's pay phone after Jack left. It'd been a long few days, and here was the pay off. I had held off calling John until the evening when I knew he would be there. I could almost see that mysterious black phone of his ringing, and it was answered very quickly.

"Hello?"

"We got our first shop."

"That was quick. I definitely picked the right man to go down there."

"Thanks. And thanks for the contracts. They helped seal the deal completely. Like drinking the smoothest drink you can imagine. By the end of the week, we should have another shop."

"Excellent. I'll call the boss and tell him."

"I decided to keep Jack on. He's a good man. You don't have to worry about him. Just wanted you to know."

"Have to go. Call me again."

I took off in my car. The air was cooler and ignited excitement in me. Then, a car swerved past me speeding, and I briefly saw Connie sitting next to me in the car. Well, not really. I realized I hadn't thought about her in the past few days. That was good. I had my work to erase her memory.

Can't bring her back. But, this was what I needed, this Florida assignment. The new experience down here, my promotion to boss. Work was the best medicine. Boy, how wise John had been to also include a change in location.

I had a little too much to drink and decided to put off going out on the town. I was elated when I arrived at my apartment. Thousands of plans rushed through my brain about how to organize the whole thing in Florida. Had to call Jack, up.

"Hello."

"Jack, I'm not interrupting your party am I."

"No, no…it won't start for about another hour or so. The wife still has the cake in the oven."

"I just realized after you left, that I want you to get started on something first thing in the morning. I decided to move my time table up. Thought about this on the way home. We need to organize a union meeting for the Tilton shop now."

"You know, I'm way ahead of you. I just talked to Jim and Buddy on the phone and told 'em to go down there and circulate."

"I want you to go down in the morning, and see this guy, Tilton. Go see him and tell him we're going to be representing the shop. Give him the run down on what he gets in return and what else could happen, if he doesn't cooperate."

"Y' know. He's known for keeping later than usual hours at his shop. I could still catch him there. My party doesn't start for a while."

"Call me back. I'm at home now."

I showered, shaved, and sat down just to close my eyes briefly. No rest for the weary. I no sooner began to fall asleep, when the phone rang.

"Hello, Tom. This is Jack."

"Hello," I said groggily, groping for my cup of coffee.

"I went over to see if Tilton was still there. He was. But he doesn't want to deal with us. Now what?"

"I see. How fast can we organize a meeting for his workers?"

"I can call in two others and send 'em to the night shift right now. That covers about one third of the plant. Jim and Buddy will be there tomorrow when the shift changes."

"Okay. Let's go for another meeting around lunchtime. Same deal. Tell the guys to circulate the announcement during their shifts. Have the girls arrange a nice platter. Invite everyone to lunch. Do we have any cards signed yet?"

"Only about twenty. And that took months to get. These guys, I told you, are easily intimidated. They don't want to lose their jobs."

"Did you get in touch with those men we almost used today?"

"Yeah. I have about fifty with maybe about another twenty that may show up."

"Okay. Tell 'em, we may start the line after lunch, sometime in the afternoon."

"Yeah, Tom. They're waiting for the word."

"Have a great birthday party. Get a good night's sleep. I'll see you tomorrow at the meeting, Jack."

"Okay. And, Tom, thank you so much for the second chance. I'll never forget how you kept me on. You ever need anything, you let me know."

"Don't worry about it. Say happy birthday to your son."

There were forty men gathered in the union hall when Jack and I entered. Jack took care of the formalities. Then, I was introduced.

"Gentlemen. My name is Thomas Furcco and I represent the BEST, the BIGGEST, and most POWERFUL UNION in this country!...I'm down from New York and I have union friends, workers like you, from all over the United States I've been working with people like you for many years. And I wanna work for YOU now! I represent the best union in the country.

"Everything that I know I've learned by experience. You don't know what experienced hands you'll be in. Nothing will go wrong. Not with me.

"The first thing I want you to know is that you must have a union in your shop. This is the sign of the times. If you don't have someone working for you in your corner, you'll be stepped on, used, and thrown away like an old pair of shoes.

"This is the only way you'll be fully protected. A union is a must for the working man, and you must realize that, or you wouldn't have made such a fine showing here today.

"You are the best at what you do. You work the hardest. Now let someone else work the hardest for you!"

"I'm not going to make a bunch of phony promises. I know you heard them before, but, I don't work that way, and neither does my union.

"This is what we can do for you. I will draw up a contract with you. What are the things you want? Better wages, overtime, sick days, vacation time, security against being fired? I will bring this contract, your demands, to your employer. He gets special contract business from us, if he says yes. That means increased business and profits for him, and better wages for you with no slow downs or threats of lay offs.

"If he doesn't agree, we sit down and talk it over. If we can't reach an understanding, we strike."

One of the men in the front row stood up and spoke.

"Sure we want a union in the shop. But our boss won't allow a union. If we agree to go on a strike, he'll fire the entire crew and just hire new workers. If we lose our jobs, where will we be?..."

"This is why you need us to represent you," I raised my voice as if in triumph.

"If anyone of you attempted to strike on your own, you would only be inviting disaster. You don't want to be the one who get hurts. A strike takes planning and experience...that's where we enter the picture.

"We are old hands at strikes. Experience is our second name. When we throw a picket line, you can believe me when I say, no one, and I mean no one and nothing will pass through. How can your boss hire someone to replace you, if they can't get through our line? It's that simple."

The man stood up again, and spoke.

"And whatta we do if the strike lasts long? How are we expected to live? How am I supposed to feed my family?"

"You right. Your families come first. But understand this, we don't ever intend to go on strike. We don't like a strike any more than you or your boss does. In the event we have to strike, this is what my union will do for you and your families. For each working day that a man stays out of the shop, the union will pay you seven dollars a day. You don't even have to walk the line…take the seven dollars a day to replace your lost salary and consider it a free vacation…on the union!"

"And win, we will. Already, Splitezer's shop has just signed up, unanimously. We even avoided a strike there. The one thing I can tell you is that in unity there is strength. The first union meeting I ever attended, the speaker there told everyone…a man is like a matchstick. One or two matchsticks in someone's hand breaks very easily. But twenty or thirty or hundred matchsticks, all together, will not break.

"I'm gonna have Jack and the men pass out some cards. If you haven't signed them already, and if you feel we're right, then sign. I'd like the refreshments served now, ladies, please over here. Have a good lunch on me, everyone…on the union. Afterwards, you should return to your shop and continue your work as usual. In the meantime, Jack and I will go see your boss and try to negotiate with him. I hope to have good news for you soon."

I raised my hand and ushered in the girls with the food and refreshments. I saw my new Florida crew passing out the cards, answering questions, showing the workers where to sign, urging the reluctant to sign as well. Workers began patting my crew on the back. I felt proud of them. Did you know that when we tallied the cards up, everyone had practically signed?

Jack sat with me in my office afterwards, as I dialed Tilton's number.

"Hello, Tilton's. Good afternoon."

"Mr. Tilton, please?"

"May I ask who's calling?"

"This is Tom Furcco."

"One moment, please."

"Hello? Who is this? Is this about the supplier?"

"Mr. Tilton, my name is Tom Furcco. I represent the union that Mr. Jack Gussona talked to you about briefly yesterday."

"I think I made my answer clear. NO. What the fuck don't you understand?"

"Mr. Tilton? We have all your men signed up. They want our union in your shop. The men are willing to strike if we don't come to some sort of agreement."

"I gave you my answer yesterday. The answer is no. I don't believe you about the workers. Now, don't fuckin' call here anymore."

The phone clicked dead.

"Jack?"

I turned to him and said, "He's still trouble...call the men we lined up. Start the picket line at Tilton's immediately. I want it big, strong and tough looking. Make sure you keep it orderly. I don't want to use any violence.

"Also send some others to mingle with the workers as they leave or arrive for their shifts. Tell the workers what happened. Give all the workers a ten dollar advance and stress the importance of their not crossing the line. Let Tilton walk right into the line when he leaves work today."

C H A P T E R   15

▼

THE FIRST BATTLE

Chapter Fifteen

I felt refreshed when I parked the car across the street from Tilton's. I studied the line and it looked solid. It would hold if it had to. Jack spotted me and started walking towards my car.

"How's it going?" I asked.

"Fine, fine. The workers are all cooperating. When they got the word that the picket line was forming outside, they all stopped working, right in the middle of the shift, and left the building."

"Great!"

"I think Tilton was trying to get in touch with you."

"I didn't get any call. Did he talk to you?"

"No, I've been too busy, organizing the line, and kept it moving and orderly."

"Yeah, we don't want trouble from the cops."

"Is he still in there?"

"Only him and the foreman."

"Let him just leave the building. Then don't let him back again."

"Y' know, Tom. I would like Buddy to be in charge of the line. He's a good union man and he won't disappoint you."

"Okay, okay. I told you to pick someone. That'll be fine. What's this? Tilton and the foreman are leaving?"

Mr. Tilton, suit and briefcase, was squeezing past the line near the office's doorway. He was furious.

"Who the hell is in charge of this?" he yelled. "I called the police!"

Jack and I started towards him.

"Are you refusing to let me into my own plant tomorrow?" he shouted approaching us.

"Are you refusing to negotiate?" I asked him.

"Yeah, you fuckin' bet I am," he said defiantly.

The police had sent three cars which were just pulling up. Mr. Tilton and his foreman turned in their direction. The patrolmen got out of their cars and surveyed the scene. Mr. Tilton walked quickly over to them and they had a little discussion. The captain just shook his head. Then, he walked over to me.

"You in charge here?"

"Yeah, I'm the union leader. We represent the shop."

"We don't want any trouble, do you understand? This is this man's plant, and you are trespassing on private property. You'll have to move."

"Jack, get all the cards," I said. "You see, we don't want any trouble either. We didn't even want this strike. Mr. Tilton has refused to sit down in arbitration and negotiate. That's the American way, you know. His workers have poor pay and bad working conditions. They live in constant fear of retaliation if they complain. We're not doing anything wrong."

"I'm sorry, you will have to leave. You cannot picket at his building and on his property without his permission. If you move your picket to the public streets, I have orders to ticket you. You will be violating a city code which prohibits anything on the public streets except for car and pedestrian traffic. It's going to be a pretty hefty fine—it's per person. You have how many picketers here already? Looks like close to a hundred."

I was trying to figure out what was going on here. Jack had said they mostly didn't bother his union. Jack had just rejoined us with the box filled with signed cards.

"Listen. Look at all these cards. Every single worker has signed them. It gives my union permission to represent them and speak for them. The picket line is legal. We're not blocking traffic on the sidewalk. Perhaps, you can talk to him. Mr. Tilton is very upset right now. But he knows the union is inevitable. Just yesterday, Splitezer's signed up with us, unanimously. They did it peaceful. No strike, no friction, no hard feelings. All we're asking is that he sit down now and talk with us. I'm sure we can reach an agreement, for everyone. You think these hard-working men want to strike? You think this isn't a pinch in their pockets? You think they wouldn't rather be back in the plant making a salary? Who's going to feed their families? Mr. Tilton is wealthy. He's got plenty in the bank to tide his family over. These men don't. Can't you have a talk with him? Just ask him to talk with us."

The captain looked at me tilting his gaze at an angle. Now I think he was wising me up. A few moments passed.

"Tell you what," he finally said. "I'm not supposed to get involved in this. But, if you agree to disperse this line entirely, and the men willingly go back into the shop and continue on with their usual work, I'll see if he'll agree to sitting down with the two of you."

The captain stepped over to the sweating Mr. Tilton and put his arm around his shoulder, took him to the side and started whispering in his ear. The line by now had stopped moving. All eyes were on me, Jack, and in another direction, the patrolman, Mr. Tilton, and the foreman. It was so quiet suddenly. Not even the breeze made a sound. All you could hear were their muffled discussion.

They talked for about twenty minutes. Then the captain waved me over. He was smiling. Mr. Tilton looked less agitated.

"Clear this area," he shouted to the workers. "And, good luck with your meeting," he said to the four of us.

"Jack, give the signal." I turned to Mr. Tilton and said, enthusiastically, "Shall we meet in about ten, fifteen minutes? In your office?"

Mr. Tilton nodded, and proceeded back into his plant as Jack climbed onto a quickly made podium of crates.

"May I have your attention? We have won the first battle! Your boss has agreed to negotiate!"

Applause, then a wave of shouts went through the line like a wave. Happy cries and relieved faces replaced the previous, anger filled ones. Some had tears in their eyes.

"Quiet...please quiet...all your boss asks is that you return to work if you're still on shift right now, and that you keep going to work as usual. This picket line is officially ended. We'll be in touch with you with good news soon!"

The crowd dispersed, parted in two almost as some returned to work and others left the area. People were patting each other on the backs with lots of talking, even some laughter.

"Shake, Jack," I said, warmly shaking his hand, over and over again. "We make a good team...who's the captain?"

"I didn't recognize him. Tom, I would've never had the balls to talk to the captain that way."

"Well, get his name. Tell him to pick a restaurant. His choice. Dinner is on the union for him and his family and friends...also slip him a fifty. Now, let's go in and work this thing out, once and for all."

One hour later, we had our contract. Tilton had officially signed up.

"Nan? Can you come in here. Bring your notebook."

The older gal at the union office, who I had first noticed the day I got here, walked and sat down opposite my desk. She crossed her legs and I studied her sharply, defined calf, and that slip of white thigh through her skirt's slit. I said to myself, oh, well, why the hell not? Maybe I should even call in the younger Jane.

"Take a letter...you'll have to look up the address as I don't have it. The name is Nancy Alder."

As she heard her name, she raised her face and then her eyes met mine.

"Dear Nancy," I continued. "I would be very pleased, if you would accept an appointment with me for this evening. Dinner and doing the town. Shall I pick you up at around eight-thirty?...And sign it, Tom."

"That won't be necessary," she said. She rose to leave, then smiled, almost giggling.

"I know the address. It's twenty-one hundred, Northwest Seventh Street. And you can call for me at around eight instead."

CHAPTER 16

▼

SEXY GALS

Chapter Sixteen

I decided after all to bring Jane with us. She was considerably younger than Nan, but a nice kid at the office. Nan was a little annoyed that Jane was invited, but very beautiful to look at, especially when I ruffled her feathers. I found out I liked annoying her. I liked the tension building. We all went for a little sightseeing, romantic drive first along the golden coastline of Miami Beach complete with an opened bottle. The brightness of all the hotels, and boat lights, and all their brilliant colors casting their images on the yacht basin's mirror of water made the view, breathtaking.

It was a sea of lights that flickered off her golden, wind swept hair, and that one's dark curls. Jane nestled against my neck from behind me in the car while Nan cuddled up close to me by my side. I gently caressed her thigh and didn't see any objections.

We pulled over at a dock and I turned around to gently kiss Jane. I played with her curls and her tongue, and gently opened a few buttons on her blouse, whispering in her ear, "later", then turned back to Nan. She pressed herself against the car door and made me lean over, almost fall towards her. The moment I touched her, I knew I had found heaven. I began to caress her more provocatively and found her locking me in the deepest kiss, hands lost all over the place finding her every curve. I was wondering if I shouldn't spend the whole weekend with this one. This one was pliable. This one could make you forget a lot of things. I am surprised we even got to the restaurant.

We dined and danced the entire evening. I only let business interfere with pleasure once. I had to use the pay phone to call John and tell him we had our second shop signed up. That was two shops in less than a week. Secrets, secrets. Boy, was he elated. And, I kept our conversation sweet and short...women, you know.

When I returned to the table, I told Nan to sit there and wait for me. I asked Jane to come outside for a minute. I winked at Nan, and leaned over to whisper in her ear, "She's leaving...you're the one." Nan smiled.

I took Jane to the back seat of the car. She was younger and she was easy. It was fun. I got a kick out of the exhibition...her clothes pushed this way and that, the undergarments half undone, flirting with a passerby seeing everything. We were both drunk and we both wanted it anyways. Nice girls down here, I thought. She wasn't the type who asked for keeps. I could tell that.

I slipped some bills down her blouse and helped her straighten her skirt. This one liked the excitement. I was an adventure for her, I realized, as she kissed me sweetly again. I asked her, if she wanted me to call her a cab? Only if I promised to see her again, she said, as I hailed her a cab, tucking my baby doll inside it safely…for later…

I returned to a very happy Nan in the restaurant.

"Why did you bring Jane?" she asked coyly.

"Oh, she's just young. Give her a break…a little excitement, a night out on the town…but, you, you're deeper…a little wiser and older, right?"

I ran my fingers through her hair as she slid her hand across my chest. We would become a spectacle soon. Already other tables were looking at us. This restaurant was seated within a large hotel overlooking the water. I asked the waiter for a phone to be brought to the table and quickly booked us a suite. Nan and I stayed the weekend at the coastline.

I couldn't wait to tell her about Jane in the car, I don't know why maybe I liked the way Nan would try to prove she was better. It must've had to do with Connie. As much as I liked Nan, I wanted to hurt her somehow. This one I liked getting angry.

Maybe I was pissed off with myself. I should be in mourning for Connie, but here I was, having a good time again. Anyway, I made Nan a tiger in bed…hadn't lost my touch. I liked the give and take. I liked it a lot. It was a wonderful weekend.

We both knew by mutual and silent agreement what we both wanted. You only had to look at how our eyes exchanged glances and we would become glued to each other. The sea breeze drifted into the room, the phone never rang to disturb us, and that's all we did…relax, call for room service, sleep, and make love, passionate love together. And not necessarily in that order, if you get my drift. We also didn't talk much. Strange, huh?

"Well, Jack. I had the best weekend of my life. Feel like a new man."

"You certainly look relaxed. Good to get that tension out of you. I tell you, I was sweating at that last picket. Came pretty close. Too close."

"Yeah. Well, here I am for another busy week of dealing. Refreshed and fit for work. Did Jane and Nan come in yet?"

"Jane's in the file room. Nan's out on a short errand…is that who's responsible? Which one?"

"Both. Let's get back to this week's agenda. Let's see the list I gave you the other day."

"I had one of the girls type it out, Tom," Jack said handing the sheet of paper to me while grinning widely.

Martins.	Creates.	William Talbut
Sanford's	Machinery	Michael Gavin
Clawton's	Clothing	Jean Commings
McCormick's	Trucking	David Armstrong
John's Brothers.	Dryers	Richard Wildder
Vestage	Clothing	Ann Sheroil

"This is what we should do," I said. "We should hit John's and McCormick's first, for without trucking and drivers the other two shops will find it difficult to operate. And John's and McCormick both have contracts with these shops. If we get 'em, we'll have about four shops signed up at once. The others will fall in line automatically.

"You should keep one man outside each shop for now with the pamphlets. Have our people inside the shops start circulating some rumors, rumors concerning a union which wants in...I want the workers aware of the fact that we're trying to put a union in their shop...just as we did with Splitezer's and Tilton's."

"Well, Tom. I think John's looks promising. Most of the workers there want a union rep. But McCormick's going to give us a little fight. There are two partners. The older one, that's McClean, seems a little scared and he'll probably see it our way soon. The younger one, Cormick is totally anti-union. We have an appointment to see him this afternoon, but, I don't think it will go well."

"Have you talked with John's already?"

"Yeah, very briefly. I explained to them how we operated with Tilton and Splitezer and they more than approved of the way we handled them. I told 'em we could give 'em the same deal. Besides, Tilton is one of their biggest contracts. They'll hate like hell to lose them."

"You know Jack, you're learning fast...we have an appointment with McCormick this afternoon?"

"Yeah at two PM."

When we went over to McCormick's shop, we were ushered into a private office that had very expensive tastes written all over it. A small man was sitting behind a large desk that almost hid him from view. I gathered this was the older partner Jack had told me about. He rose from his seat and extended his hand to me.

"You must be Mr. Furcco. I have already met your associate…Mr. Gussona…I'm Bob McLean."

"How do you do, Bob, may I? Please call me Tom."

"I understand you want us to sign up with your union, is that right?"

"Yeah, Bob."

"I'm having difficulty with my partner John, John Cormick. That's how we got the idea of this shop. We used the "Mc" from my name, and the "Cormick" from his. Get it, McCormick?

"That's very nice, Bob. But what's the trouble with your partner? Don't you have the controlling interest in the shop?"

"No, I don't. Neither of us do. John and I are partners all the way down the line, fifty-fifty. As far as John is concerned, he's stubborn and independent. He doesn't like anyone telling him what to do."

"Well, Bob. I'm pretty sure you can persuade your partner to see things your way. Talk to him. Tell him it will be very beneficial if he accepts our union. I can assure you that all of our promises are not empty ones. You'll be rich soon.

"We can show him proof. Every shop we represent has had an increase in business and volume. Our union has practically handed this to them on a silver platter. Is your partner so independent that he'd turn his back on all these extra contracts we can get for you? Think of all the extra money we can give you with no strings attached and he's really gonna just throw it down the drain? What kind of business man is he?"

Bob sat there silently. He began to shake his head.

"I'll talk to him again. That's all I can say. Nothing may come of it."

This had not gone the way I wanted. That John Cormick was going to fuck us up. I could tell. And that Bob, didn't have enough balls inside him. I didn't think he could swerve his stubborn partner at all.

This was my first big problem since I arrived in Florida. And, I didn't like it one bit. The other shops wouldn't sign if I couldn't get Mr. Cormick to buckle. My biggest ace in the hole was to stop their trucking. If they couldn't ship, their production would be halted. Then they would have to sign. But no, that bastard, Cormick, is the one supplying them with the trucks. How was I gonna put a stop to this and fast?

"I was thinking of throwing up a picket line. Wonder if that would spoil things? The old man wants to come in with us. But if I thrown in some pressure, he might rebel and decide to fight us too. Whattaya think, Jack?"

"I heard the old man is highly respected by the employees there. They'll back him all the way. If he joins his younger partner—"

"Yeah, yeah, we'll really have a fight on our hands. No, I have something much better planned for our Mr. Cormick."

I picked up the phone to buzz Nan.

"Nan, will you see if your can find Buddy Sambino, Jim Larosa, and, how about, Jane...Jane Dwyer? When you locate them, send them into my office.

"Jack, I'm going to do something. There are six shops at stake and we can't afford to let one bastard stop us from organizing them. Remember no questions asked."

"Come off it, Tom. I'm a union man, just like you. When I joined I said I'd go all the way to the end of the street and I meant that. So count me in. Besides you just made me your under boss."

There was a knock on the door. Buddy, Jim and Jane walked in.

"Sit down." I said.

"I don't want any questioning, hesitating, refusing, or anything. Just follow my orders."

They nodded and said yes.

"Alright then, this is the full story. We're working on six shops right now, kind of all at once. One shop is fuckin' us up. This shop would be ours except for one man who's busting our balls. He's the cause of all our problems. We've tried persuasion, but now my patience has been exhausted. We need to resort to more drastic measures.

"Now, here's his photo. Pass it around. I want you to study it so that you will know him when you see him. He's about five foot nine, weighs about one hundred and seventy pounds, has brown hair, and as you can see, his face is pock-marked. There's a tattoo on his right arm and he likes wearing fancy clothes.

"He hangs out in a joint over on Northwest Seventy-Ninth and Eleventh Avenue. It's called Sam's. It's known to be a hangout for quite a few girls. He likes his women and he likes variety. He figures himself a real ladies' man, but I think it's his bank roll which is more attractive. So this is where you come in, Jane. You dress real pretty and sexy tonight. You're going to meet him tonight."

"Make a play for him and get him to pick you up and bring you home. He's easy. All you have to do is slobber all over him. Wear something very low cut and a dress with a few slits. Make sure he gets to see a little something, get it? You know how you ladies like to tease a guy. Tease him."

"Okay. But am I supposed to go all the way with him...you know...am I?"

"You have nothing to worry about. I'm not putting you in the lion's den. Buddy will be with you at all times. He'll tag behind you to Cormick's place."

"Now, Buddy, I want you in that bar before she arrives. When she enters the place, don't let her out of your sight for one minute. When they leave, he won't be paying attention if you're following. He'll only have one thing on his mind with Jane, especially after a few drinks...now, if he heads to a motel, you—Jane, have to get suddenly sick or something. Twist an ankle if necessary, but don't go to any motel. This will only work if he takes you home with him. Got it?"

"Yes," they both said.

"Great. And Buddy, if for some reason, Jane can't get away from him and he heads to a motel, you may have to stage something. Run into his car or something. Alright? Now, Cormick usually goes to Sam's about nine. Buddy, get there about eight thirty. Jane, walk in about nine fifteen. Okay?"

"Sounds good. But what do I do when I get to his house?" Jane asked.

"Nothing. Absolutely nothing. Just go with the flow when you get inside his house. Buddy and Jim will be in soon to get you outta there. Jack, go out and make sure that Cormick came into his office today and that he's not away or something? Jim, you stay I wanna talk to you."

"Isn't this exciting, Buddy?" Jane got up. Everyone shuffled out of the office except for Jim.

"Jim. I've heard Jane is pretty easy. Is it true?"

"Just between you and me, she has been with practically everyone here. Even with the married ones. She's a lot of fun."

"Yeah, I thought so. What about Nan?"

"She's had a few. But she's more secretive. I don't think she bothers with married men unless he has a lot of dough."

"But Jane will screw anybody?"

"Probably."

"I also heard you know how to pick locks, Jim. Is that right?"

"You sure hear a lot of things. And keep this between our ears?"

"Sure. When Jane gets to Cormick's house, you join up with Buddy. After you know they're in bed together, and obviously, occupied, get in there. I want you and Buddy to surprise them. Slap little Jane's ass and get her dressing and packing. Give her one of your car keys. I don't want Cormick to know she knows you.

"Then work Cormick over. Make it bad enough to land him in the hospital, but not dead, see? Be quick, don't wake the neighbors. That's why I don't want them going to a hotel. Walls are thin there and someone might hear you. But in a big fancy house, there's more of a buffer. Ransack the house a little. Make it look like some nigger's robbed the place"

"Should I catch up with Buddy before tonight, or are you going to fill him in?"

I buzzed Nan. "You can fill Buddy in. Nan, Can you get Jane in here again?"

When Jane walked in, I told her to shut the door. I went over to her and held her in my arms kissing her quickly. I whispered in her ear.

"Would you do me a little favor? Give Cormick a good time after all. I need him occupied with you in bed so Buddy and Jim can break into his house. Pretend you don't know Buddy and Jim when they break in on you. They'll give you a car key and you can just leave. But, I need you to keep him occupied. You can come to my place afterwards. And here…" I pushed some bills down her dress.

"I can't trust anyone else. He'll be putty in your hands."

"That's alright, Tom. Leave Cormick to me. I'm your girl. I love to follow orders. See you later."

EXECUTION

Chapter Seventeen

Jane knocked on the door. It was close to midnight.

"Hi! Can I have a drink?"

"Hi beautiful. Help yourself. How did everything go?"

"It was easier than you think. He gave me all this money to go home with him, but Cormick drank too many. I had to practically drag him into his house. He conked out immediately. I just baby sat until Buddy and Jim got in."

"You left as soon as they got there?"

"Yep."

"I haven't heard from 'em. I don't like it. Tell you what, Jane—make yourself at home or here's some money for a cab if you don't feel like staying. I'm going out to find 'em."I quickly grabbed my jacket and keys. This was a risky and dangerous assignment, and now I was wondering if something had backfired. The streets were deserted except for an occasional car. I headed first to the union office.

I called Jack at home. He volunteered to drive by Buddy's and Jim's to see if they had gone home. I decided to drive past Cormick's, but the street was quiet. No police even. That was a good sign. Well, maybe they went out drinking afterward. No telling where they could be.

I went back to the office and waited to hear from Jack. His call came in about an hour later. There was still no sign of them. I told Jack I would be home if he had any news.

Jane was asleep when I got there. I had my usual Jack Daniels and had not realized I had fallen asleep, I was awakened by the constant ringing of the phone. I jumped as a slip of Connie raced through me all tangled up in half-asleep and half-remembered dreams. I shook it off and forced myself awake. Jane softly moaned besides me. Picking up the receiver, I heard Buddy's voice.

"Tom?"

"Buddy? What the fuck happened. Are you two okay? I was worried. Expected to hear from you before now."

"Everything is fine. We're both fine. The assignment was easy.

"We decided to drive outta the city. I have a small bungalow outside of Miami. We thought it was better to drive straight through and keep as much distance between us and Cormick's, just in case. We're just having some coffee at an all night diner. This is the first chance I got to pay phone you."

"Damn it. Next time let me know beforehand. Jack and I went out looking for you. We thought that you got pinched or even whacked."

"I'm sorry. It was a last minute decision."

"Well, go get a sun tan, and take a day or two off. You've earned it. I'll be giving you an extra envelope for this."

I hung up the phone and slept like a baby with a baby doll in my arms. Two days later, the Miami Herold ran something on Cormick. It was buried on page three:

> *John Cormick, a local trucking owner, was found by his cleaning woman at his home in Coral Gables. He was badly beaten and unconscious when rushed to the hospital. He was listed in fair condition and is expected to make a full recovery. Details of his exact injuries were not released, or how long he will be at the hospital. Apparently, he did not see his assailants. His home was ransacked and the police have said that robbery was the motive...*

Smooth, I thought. Smooth as velvet.

By magic, word seemed to spread about what happened to Cormick. Martin's signed up with us first. A week later Vestage signed, then Clawton. We had gained three of the shops out of the original six we had planned to organize.

I was elated and so was Jack. He may not have approved of all my methods, but he was happy with the results. Unfortunately, McCormick's still hadn't signed. I wasn't too worried. It was only a matter of time before we would see that name on the dotted line.

Jack and I decided not to approach him until he was out of the hospital. I shouldn't have waited. He certainly lost no time. From his very hospital bed, we found out he had conversed at length with John's and Stanford's and they decided to merge. Now I had lost three shops.

What was with this prick? He knew why he was assaulted and we figured he'd be putty in our hands afterwards. We had counted ourselves in, as far as his shop was concerned, we were certain he'd be over-anxious to join us. Was this man a complete asshole? He was determined to fight me, wasn't he? He knew the merger would fuckin' hurt me, didn't he?

Things began to backfire. Buddy, Jim and Jack were all attacked within one week by unknown assailants. Thankfully their injuries were minor. Jane packed her bags and left to go stay with an out of town relative. I told Nan to do the same. In fact, all the girls were told to take their vacation time and disappear for a while. Some of our union spies, who had gotten jobs in other shops, were found out and fired. On top of that, McCormick refused to truck for any of the shops we had signed up.

I had had it with Mr. Cormick. I threw up picket lines around all three shops but Cormick must have found some muscle and goons. They arrived out of the blue and attacked us. Each day the line turned into a mini-riot.

By the time the fight was in its seventh week, everyone was hurting. I recalled my valiant speech I had given at the union hall. I had the confidence of every man there. No promise would go unfulfilled...now, all the promises, every declaration seemed to be back-firing and going down the drain. What had happened to all the work and protection I had promised them?

They stayed on my back and kept asking me those questions. I knew it would only be a matter of time before the workers would turn against us too. Then everything we had done and were doing would be a lost cause. Something had to be done soon. Something drastic...

I called up John in New York.

"Hello?"

"Hi."

"Tom, you son of a bitch, how the hell are you?"

"I'm okay. I need your help."

"What? Has something come up? I heard about that prick Cormick. Someone should do a repeat with him, if you get what I mean. But aside from that, they're spreading a lot of good things about you up here. Your turning into a really good earner."

"I don't know what you've heard. I need to know if Sallie is free?"

"Probably. Why? You want him?"

"Yeah. The sooner the better. It's urgent. Could he get down here in a day or two?"

"You've been having a rough time down there for the last couple of months, but you're doing a wonderful job. Tell you what. If Sallie isn't free, I'll make him free. Look for him to arrive in two days. And a word of advice, Tom. Think before you fuckin' act."

"I know. Thanks."

Two days later, I waited at the office to hear that Sallie had just gotten off the plane. Did I know what I was doing? Should I have asked for him? My hands were tied, and there was only one thing left to do. They sent me down to organize shops and that's exactly what I was going to do. I could not sit back idly while one man destroyed all I had built up. I couldn't permit one wise ass to prevent me from doing my job.

There was a knock on the door.

"Sallie! You son of a bitch, how the hell are you?"

"If you let go of me, you son of a bitch, and let me breathe, I'll be fine. Tom, you look great!"

I released him and took a good look at him.

"You haven't changed much Sallie. How is Sheila?"

"She couldn't be better. She said hello by the way. Misses not seeing you."

"Well, Sallie, this is like old times and it calls for a drink. But first, I want you to meet Jack. I'd be lost without him."

I opened my door and waved Jack in.

"Jack, I want you to meet the best friend I ever had. He's taking a little vacation and thought he'd stop by to say hello. We go back a long time in New York. Now, let's all go get that drink."

We had a few rounds of drinks. Jack stayed for a while, but I knew he'd make up some excuse and leave. He knew we had a lot to discuss, especially old times, and we did.

"You're doing a great job down here, Tom. We get nothing but good reports concerning you."

"Yeah, what do they say about this damn mess I'm in now?…"

"Look, Tom. This is to be expected. John told you that this was a hard place to crack. Or he wouldn't have sent you down here to begin with. The New York office knows you can handle this. Don't be so damn hard on yourself."

"Maybe I am, Sallie. But I have to. In fact, I want to."

"Are you sure you're not burying yourself in this work to forget Connie?"

"Maybe. Work is good for me. Connie was the kind of girl you never forget. The rest of 'em, they're good for fun and a diversion, but it's not the same thing. But enough, Sallie. I have a problem, a big one and I need your help…"

"What do you think friends are for? What's up?"

"Well, listen to what I have to say and what I want you to do before you commit yourself. Let's not talk here. Let's go to your hotel room."

We arrived there and I began outlining things for Sallie. I told him about all the shops I had organized, the strikes, the operation, the works. Then, I got to Cormick, the bastard that was fucking up my plans.

"Instead of roughing him up, I should've just wasted him. Then with just the old man left, we could've easily gotten McCormick signed up. He's a real thorn in my damn ass now."

"Why don't you just hit him hard? Close down his shop? Find a different trucking firm for your other shops?"

"I probably made a big error in delaying striking his plant. Now, it's too late. He's managed to sway two other shops to his side of the fence. Now they're playing my fuckin' game. They're beginning to refuse to do business with any of the shops I have. It can't go on too much longer like this."

"Does he have any family, friends?"

"No. Just some lady friends. I can't get to him that way. Roughing him didn't turn him around. Jack has contacted him and offered the best deal, but he won't listen. Money and fear don't work."

"How about any bad habits…gambling…y' know?"

"No, this kid's clean as a whistle. He likes his ladies, but with no wife, who would I blackmail? We've asked him what he wants. His answer is NOTHING. He doesn't want a damn thing…so, Sallie. We're good friends. We've been through a lot together. You're the only one I'd ever say this to. I'm desperate. I've hashed and rehashed this whole mess and I've come to one conclusion. This has to be an outside job.

"I'm too well known down here as the union organizer. I'm watched all the time. I can't say for sure I could get away with it, even if I did the job myself. And I cannot let the union become openly involved."

Sallie shot me a quick, stern glance. His old familiar expression told me he knew exactly what I had in mind. For a few, brief minutes, the room was absolutely silent.

"He has to meet with a fatal accident. He has to be whacked."

"Tom, are you sure you have tried everything?"

"Yeah, I'm sure. I have racked my brains for some kind of solution. The other shops are at my ass constantly, and it will only be a matter of weeks before they'll be forced to close their doors. I can't let that happen.

"Too much is at stake. Possibly millions of dollars to the union eventually, and I'm not gonna let one young bastard ruin it. I'm running out of solutions and time, especially time.

"Sallie, you're the only person I can turn to. Can you do it?"

"Won't the police assume the union had something to do with it?"

"Of course, they will. But, you have no connections here. They won't be able to tie us together. If an investigation does wind up at the union's doorstep, I'll make sure that the whole crew has an airtight alibi. I can reach some of the right people as long as the price is right. No, Sallie, the union has nothing to fear if he's eliminated."

Again, the room was silent.

"Alright Tom. I'm your man."

I opened my briefcase.

"This is all the information on Cormick. Read it. It's everything we could get our hands on. There's one thousand dollars here and an unmarked gun. After this is taken care of, you should take the next flight out and disappear. Give me a pay phone call when you are back in New York. And Sallie, this is another time I'm indebted to you. If you ever need me, just call."

"Okay. I'm solo, you understand. I'll be leaving this hotel immediately. You won't be able to find me. You won't know anything until after it's done."

"I understand. Thank's Sallie."

Two days later the newspaper read:

This morning, a body of a man was found floating in the Tamiami canal. At first glance, it appeared to be an accidental drowning. Upon closer examination, two bullets, lodged in his temple, were found. The coroner has not released his full report yet. The body was identified as John Cormick, of...McCormick, a local trucking company. The police are not giving out any further information. There was no apparent motive for the killing and a formal statement will be forthcoming.

CHAPTER 18

▼

GOING HOME

Chapter Eighteen

This was the vilest thing I done since the war, with maybe the exception of cutting up Connie's killer. I had ordered someone's murder. I hated myself. I didn't expect to, but I did.

Once more, I returned to the bottle. I felt nothing for anyone. I could justify what happened to Connie's killer. It was personal. That man took something from me that I could never get back. But here, I actually paid for someone's murder. There was nothing personal involved this time. Had I hit a new low from the gutter to the sewer?

I could, of course, talk myself into this. Come on, Tom, think hard. You had a job to do and had no other alternative. There was too much at stake, too much to lose. You gave him every chance in the books. Is it your fault that he was an asshole? Why didn't the stubborn son of a bitch heed my warnings? Why did he force my hand?

Because he thought he was stronger and in the right. Well, he was neither. But, still my conscience wrestled. I should've listened to Connie. She said get out. Had I not gone on that last assignment before her death…and just dragged us both out of there, she would still be alive.

Who had I become? If I pulled out of the union, had I gone too far already? Wasn't this a permanent entanglement with no escape?…All these thoughts crowded my brain. Look at how I had treated Jane and Nan. Well, maybe it was different with women. Maybe, that's how it will always be. No Connie, no deal, right God? I don't think for a minute that I will ever let someone close to me again. They're there for the show now. All dressed up pretty, and you can have a lot of fun. But, I've lost so much. I think that's all I want now, just the show and the fun, and my favorite panacea, my old friend, Jack Daniels.

Perhaps, that's why this was so easy. Of course, I knew I would never have to do the dirty deed myself. But, it was better this way. I was becoming harder and crueler. After Connie's death, I became unemotional of my feelings. That's what they wanted you know. The union had no place for someone with no balls. I could still get out if I wanted, get out completely and escape from this mess…

I had broken into offices and files, stolen and spied, lied to others about who I was to get a job, blown up machines like a terrorist, beaten someone into a pulp, cut someone up into pieces for Connie, sold a woman almost into prostitution, and now I had ordered a paid, contract. The problem was, it bothered me. It bothered me too much...I could still get out...yes, I'll do just that...

"Hi Jack," I said walking into the office. "What's new?..."

"Oh, good news. John's and McCormick's signed up...John Cormick's body was found floating in the canal last week..." Jack paused and glanced up at me in a strange way. "Tom, you wouldn't be in some kind of jam, would you?... If you are, and you need any help, you can always count on me."

"I know I can, Jack, but you're way off track. I'm not in any way involved in his death, but I'm mighty glad he's off my ass. His death sure cleared up a lot of our problems. Blessing in disguise."

"The police are investigating, you know, and I'm expecting a visit from them. I did hear that since he was such a lady's man, and chased so many women, he probably finally ran into a love spurned girl or a jealous boyfriend or husband. That's my best bet on who did him in."

"Jack, if the police do decide to give us a little visit, you talk to 'em. I wasn't around. In fact, I put on a little buzz over the past week and many people have seen me. No, Jack, I have an airtight alibi.

"In fact, I never met Cormick. Never been in his company, nothing. I was nowhere near him when it happened. No one can tie me in with Cormick, and no one from our union would be involved in something so vile as murder. We negotiate. Remember that. Make sure the police understand how we operate...a girl or a jealous husband...how about that?...Well, it's no skin off our ass...

"By the way, how come Sanford hasn't signed with us?"

"I don't know, Tom. One minute he was ready to sign, and then he reneged. I think we should put a little more pressure on him and tighten the picket line. Maybe then, he'll see things our way..."

"That's good, Jack. That's what I like to hear. You have really come a long way since I took you under my wing. In fact, that makes it a little easier for me now. I'm giving you back your old job as boss here."

"No, Tom, I don't want it like that. We're a team. We should work together."

"No, Jack, I'm afraid not. I took you under my wing so you would learn the rules and how the business should operate and I'm convinced you can handle the job. I'm going back to New York. And I deserve that."

"I'm sorry, Tom. Well, no, I'm happy for you if that's what you want. I guess this is good-by?"

"We'll be seeing each other until we get everything in order. But I wanted you to know first."

"Thanks, Tom. You taught me a lot. I'll never forget you."

"Same here, pal."

I decided to return to the town where I had married. The town of so many years of happiness. It hadn't changed much. A few new buildings, a few new faces, but in general, it was the same town I had left. Even my old friends seemed the same. Yes, the town and the people were as they always had been. There was one thing different, however, but I couldn't put my finger on it right away. Eventually, I did…it wasn't the people or the town, it was me.

All my friends were still living the same sort of life they always had. They had their jobs and their families…their white picket fences and neat little lawns. How ironic, when I got the real live, picket line instead?

In general, they were contented with their lives, but they were dull lives. This is where I knew I had changed. Once I was just like them, but after working for the union, I didn't fit in here. These were peaceful, law abiding citizens with their little, repetitious routines. But, I liked adventure. I thrived excitement. And look what I had as a life. I was corrupt and lawless. I was changed, and yet, here I was, determined to become one of them again. Was it possible? Could I hide my past? Could I change myself? Could I hide from the union?

I loafed around for a while. I had plenty of money so I didn't have to go to work. But, I became bored. I tried to forget my short lived career in the union, but I still reminisced. It was great when I was in charge of something, giving the orders, reeling in the shops and the money. I was about ready to toss in this town…this town and its ways belonged to average people, and I wasn't one of them. Then, I met Joan…

A certain tavern became my favorite hangout, and I spent a great deal of time there. When you first walked in, the thing that caught your eye immediately was the small pool table. On the right was a mahogany bar that started in a semi-circle, then ran the length of the room, some forty or so feet. There was a shuffle board to your left, a juke box behind the booths, and in the center of the room, a dance floor. In the day, the room was lit up by an enormous skylight. At night, there were only the discreet, little lamps on the walls and candles on the table.

Joan, a married lady, was the owner. I walked in one night and as I went towards the rear of the room, I spied her. She was sitting in a booth with two other girls and two men. She laughed. It was her laughter that first attracted me to her. It rang out across the dance floor over the sounds of the band. It was contagious. It was gay laughter and it filled me with warmth and happiness to hear someone laugh so innocently and sincerely.

When she stood up I was surprised to see she was so tall, about five feet eight in heels. Her hair was blond and silky, and she wore a well-fitted blue suit that showed all her curves. I watched her dancing for a long while, and began wondering about the color of her eyes.

I wanted to dance with her, but for some reason, I just watched. I couldn't tell if she was with someone special. There also was a wedding ring on her finger. After a couple straight shots of Jack Daniels, I finally strode to her table.

"Do you care to dance?" I asked her.

"Well, I usually don't dance with the customers. But you're a regular, aren't you? I'll make an exception...my name is Joan."

"I'm Tom."

We walked out onto the dance floor and I took her gently in my arms. The softness of her body melted in my arms as we whirled across the dance floor. She swayed and moved with rhythm as I held her. It seemed her body almost belonged to mine. I wouldn't let go looking into her deep, brown eyes. She was causing a disturbance in me that I had not expected. She could feel it too. She almost trembled.

"Would you have a drink with me? Let me get a table," I said quickly.

"If you had a table, I might sit for just one drink. But, I see you don't have one..."

"Let me talk to the waitress—" She interrupted me with that laughter again.

"Don't you know who I am? I own this place...a table I can get you very easily."

She waved to one of the waitresses who came over. Within a few minutes a new table was put out and set.

"Come over here, Tom. We can sit here."

We talked and talked and talked, about everything and anything. And we drank and we danced and time seemed of no importance. She told me she was married but not working on it. It had gone bad a long time ago and now it was just a formality. I told her about myself, but not the union. I talked about my plans for the future. I lightened up a little inside.

It was nice suddenly. To talk to a woman for a change…to laugh with her. Not one of those youngsters or diversionary tactic girls. I wasn't lonely anymore. Except she was married. What would come of that—a one night's pleasure? Well, here was the adventure. I decided to see her again. I even insisted on seeing her home. We only stole a kiss at her doorway. It lasted a very long time, but, she agreed to see me the next night.

She didn't show. Did I ever take a fall. It was like I landed somewhere with my breath kicked out from under me. I looked up her number and called her desperately.

A man answered.

"Can I speak to Joan, please?"

"This is her husband. What the hell do you want?"

"Nothing," I said as I hung up.

That's what you get Tom. You thought everything was going to be wonderful just because you meet a woman and you're attracted to her. You think she's different and like someone you have never met before and then she lies to you right off the bat. But this is all in your own stupid head. She really doesn't care about you. You're like any other guy in that bar to her—nothing. You just don't fit in here.

You can pretend you're going to forget all about the union but it's not going to happen, is it? These people in this town belong here, but you don't. I don't even know why I wasted so much time coming back here. This is stupid. I just can't loaf all my life, and be at some dame's beck and call.

There is a place where you belong, Tom. You should give it another chance. The union isn't that bad. It pays your bills for you, doesn't it? At least with the union, a man's a man and a woman's a woman, and they can always be relied upon no matter how demanding the situation. They're hard and tough, but soft and gentle. Those are your people, Tom. You should go back. I really only needed a good long break and to get away from the Florida bullshit. That's all I really needed. Now I can return because there's really nothing here for me. I was wrong. I missed the union.

"Hello, Tom!" Pat said as I entered the reception room.

"Hi, is John in?"

"Yes, he is. Walk right in. You know the way."

As soon as John saw me, he leaped out of his chair and grabbed me in a hug and kissed me on both cheeks.

"Tom, you son of a bitch. How the hell are you?"

He was still shaking my hand and wouldn't let go.

"I'm just fine, John. I needed a little of my own time...But I'm kind of restless now and I want to get back to work."

"Well, have a seat. Where did you go when you left Florida? We got your final reports, and then nothing. Hell, we began to think you had been whacked or something?"

"John, I just need to get out of Florida. Just for a while. After that mess in Florida, I just needed to wrap it all up. But y' know, it's like a shot of coke. Once the shot wears off, you have to come back for another one. It's union fever, excitement and action I need again. And I'm one of your best earners and you know it."

"Tom, you know that certain things have to be done regardless of how unpleasant. We can't change that. You may hate yourself for a while, you may want to get out from under, but it's in your blood...the union. He's always connected here and leaves his conscience behind.

"I knew you'd return. You sure are a sight for sore eyes and boy, am I glad to see you. I have something...it might be what you're looking for...and yes, as far as I'm concerned, you're still the best earner for us.

"They need a man in New Orleans. I don't know the complete story. What I can gather is that they're having some sort of trouble with a man down there and don't know quite how to handle it. You can take it blind if you want. Then, there's one more opening in Puerto Rico..."

"No, John, no fuckin' Puerto Rico. I don't know the language. How long will that job last in New Orleans? Y' know?"

"No, I don't, Tom. I don't know anything much about the job. You'll have to get in touch with a man called Sid Ragosea. He has an office on Canal Street in New Orleans.

"One more thing. Be careful, like I always say. Put Florida behind you. It all worked out anyways. And no more damn disappearing acts, okay?"

"You got it. Don't worry, John. I'll see you when I get back."

New Orleans, the Big Easy. I could feel it. Warm and hot and spicy.

CHAPTER 19

▼

FAT BOY

Chapter Nineteen

I caught a flight to New Orleans and checked into a hotel under the name of John Peters. I decided to use a false name because of the Florida execution. My room gave me a wonderful view of the crescent city as New Orleans was called. The city was still surrounded by a moat which had protected it from attack for centuries. I could see Canal Street from my window. It was the largest street in the world, and viewing it from seventeen floors up, I believed it.

Both sides of the street were the width of Times Square. In the center were two trolley tracks, and at one end were the docks to the ferry. From there you could sail to Algiers and Lake Poncentrain. Shops lined both sides of the streets and it reminded me a little of New York City. There was also the famous French Quarters where it was widely rumored you could find anything your heart desired, providing you could pay the price. New Orleans was a fun town, but I had business to do.

I located Ragosea's address in the phone book. I left a message, returned to my hotel, and ordered some Jack Daniels with ice. I made my drink and settled down on the balcony. Then there was a knock at the door.

A tall, thin man about thirty-five walked into the room. This was a powerful built man about two hundred and fifty pounds thick dark hair brushed straight back. The real tough guy look.

"You must be John Peters?"

"And you must be Sid Ragosea."

I reached into my wallet, took out my new identification card with my false name, as he reached for his. Both of us were satisfied.

"Now what's this about? I'm in the dark as to what this job is."

"It's like this. In the last six months I've lost two of my crew. The first one was found floating in the gulf. He had two fuckin' bullets through his head. That was about six months ago."

"Two months ago, another crew member was blasted with machine gun fire as he was leaving his home. His wife also caught some of it, and though she's still alive, she says it happened too fast. She didn't see a thing."

"She didn't even get a glimpse of the killer?" I asked anxiously.

"No, she couldn't help us in the slightest. A car went past the house taking everything in its sight. That's all she knows."

"Don't you have any clues at all?..."

"John, we've racked our brains trying to find out who's behind this and why. We have it narrowed down to two things. Although we're having a little union trouble, this isn't an outside job. We think its someone local."

He paused in his speech and remained quiet. I waited and then nothing. Finally, I said, "You said two clues. What's the second one?"

"It seems that every time one of my men was hit, a certain man was spotted in the vicinity. It isn't strong enough evidence, but that's all we have to go on right now. Y' know, I'm just grabbing at straw's right now."

"No, no. That's alright. What's the guy's name?"

"His name is Virgel Attkins. He conveniently was seen leaving town after every one of 'em were whacked. We have a line on him, but not much so far. He's originally from Cleveland and has a rap-sheet that isn't pretty to look at. He was indited for murder once, but let off due to lack of evidence.

"He's been know to kill before, but we don't think he's ever hired himself out...I just can't figure out, why our crew?...None of 'em have ever been to Cleveland. Neither of 'em knew each other outside of the office...and the main thing I'm concerned about now is that this man, Attkins, is back in town."

"Well, Sid. If you know the bastard gunned your men down, why don't you just take care of him?"

"That's just it. We aren't sure it's him. If we whack 'em, and someone else in my crew gets it, then what? Then we've fuckin' wasted him for no reason and we still won't know who the assassin is. And, what if he's linked to whoever is behind all this? Can't question a dead man, can we?...No, we have to catch the son of a bitch somehow red-handed. Then we can whack him."

"Hold on, Sid. You said kill him, right? Gun him down, blast him. If it comes to killing, you can count me out. Let's get one thing straight. I'm no triggerman. I was sent down here to help you. I'll tail him for you if that's what you want. Let's find out who he is and what he's after. I'll even drive the car for the finale...but I won't pull the trigger. I'm no damn killer..."

"John, I need your fuckin' help. I sent up to New York for help. When they told me they were sending you, I was more than glad and still am. It will be a pleasure to work with someone like you. You have such an outstanding record, but you must understand. I can't put any of my men on this job. And I can't trust a wino or drug addict or even a stupid ass nigger. I will have to do it myself..."

"Just so that you understand where my boundaries are, Sid. I can drive, plan, analyze, but you're on your own about any killing."

"Fair enough."

"Now, Sid, the first thing I need is all the information you have on your man, description, habits, etc., any and all information that you have concerning him. Also find out if anyone has even the most remote idea why these men were killed or why this man could be the killer. Get me all that shit and let me go over it. We'll also send it to the New York office and see if they come up with anything. Maybe they can dig up something on him."

"Okay. Give me a few hours and I'll have that all together for you. You should change hotels when I leave. Don't stay near here. How about we meet up in about an hour?"

"Where?"

"How about near the ferry?"

He left quickly, and I threw my things into my bag and left as well. I was soon in a new hotel, pondering our conversation, as the hour was nearly up.

I was surprised to see a union boss driving a battered, beat up Buick.

"Get in," Sid said.

"Plenty power beneath this baby's hood, huh?"

"Never failed me yet."

We drove down Canal Street heading for Lake Poncentrain. Sid slowed down the car as we neared a certain house. Two men were sitting on the porch.

"The one on the left."

The man on the left was fat, and jolly looking. He must've weighed close to three hundred pounds. He didn't look alarming or dangerous at all, until he turned his head. He had probably been born with an ugly expression, but what made it even worse, was a busted nose and a long, purplish scar which ran from his eye to his chin. There was a look of a killer written all over him.

"Fat Boy," I murmured.

Our car passed his house and Sid said, "What'd you say?"

"Fat Boy. That's what he reminds me of. Who's the guy with him?"

"They pal around. I don't think he's anyone special."

"So what's the plan here? Should we just tail him for a good week or so?"

"Okay. Do you mean round the clock?"

"Yeah. We need a different car. He's already seen this one pass by his house. He'll get suspicious if he sees it again...what's around here? Is there any place we can go and still be able to watch his house? Or is there some place safe we can hide in?"

"I don't think so. Let me get someone to check out who lives around here. If someone's away, maybe we can break in and set up shop there. Our best bet is to wait from a distance when he leaves his house, and follow as loosely as possible without him noticing."

And so we did. We did locate a vacant house within sight of his and it wasn't too hard to get in. But all this was to no avail. He acted as if he was a tourist on the town. Both he and his pal reveled all the time in the French Quarters, hitting a different bar almost every night. Once there, they never made an attempt to leave until early morning. Once home, it was mostly sleep. Once a day, however, the fat boy would take a drive by himself, and would always manage to pass by Sid's office.

We noticed they didn't get excessively drunk. They always seemed to have their wits about them. They didn't pick up any women and seemed to be mostly interested in the floor show. They talked mostly to each other or, occasionally, to a bartender. Very secretive.

In those crowded places, it was very hard for them to spot us. I don't think he was aware that we were shadowing him. However, after a week of this steady tailing, we were ready to back off.

"So, whattaya think, John?"

"Bit of a puzzle. Y' know if they were normal tourists, men on vacation with lots of money to burn, they would be really living it up. They would go for the girls, rent hotel rooms, mix with the crowds, and literally have a ball."

"Maybe they're queer."

"Maybe they're on some sort of assignment and that means no women, no distractions. I don't like that he drives by your fuckin' office at least once a day."

"That may be coincidental because we're on the main street. Even a tourist on a sightseeing tour would drive up and down Canal Street."

"Could you pretend to move your office? If he finds the new place, and starts driving by it, it's not coincidence then, is it?"

"I don't know. That would take a bit of planning. Let me think about it."

"I still say they have a definite purpose in their innocent looking actions and it's not sightseeing."

We had tailed "Fat Boy" from his house. He had stopped on Canal Street near Sid's union office. One of Sid's crew walked out and sure enough, "Fat Boy" pulled behind him and stayed with him. We were parked about seven or eight car lengths away, and began following him. It might be coincidence, but after driving a few blocks, I was sure it wasn't.

"Who's he following, Sid?"

"That's Bob Dunti. I don't know why…Dunti's only been with our crew for about eight months."

"Well, at the moment there doesn't seem to be a reason or connection. Could something have happened say last year, that they're going to have it out now?"

"I wish the hell I knew what this was all about. I don't need another one of my crew taken out…Christ, it's a pain in the ass."

"I agree. It's bad enough having trouble to begin with, but when you don't know the reason why?…"

We continued trailing "Fat Boy" who stayed faithfully behind Bob the whole time until Bob reached his home. As Bob parked his car, our man slowed down considerably and I could see that "Fat Boy" was memorizing the address and taking in the surrounding landscape. We continued following "Fat Boy" back to his house.

"Listen, Sid. This is serious. The bastard knows where one of your crew lives. Does he have a family?"

"Yeah, I think so."

"I don't want our car seen near Bob's house now that "Fat Boy" has the address. Call Bob, and tell him, to come right down to the office."

"But he just left there."

"Just fuckin' tell him, it's important. Can you put someone else on watching "Fat Boy" at his house for the rest of today? He usually doesn't go out again until nightfall."

"Okay, okay. I'll get Tony on that. He's still at the office."

We pulled up about two blocks away from Sid's office. I got out and went round the back so no one would see we were together. Sid met up with me inside. Tony was told to go watch "Fat Boy's" house, no questions asked, and left in a hurry. The office felt the invisible tension, as if some sort of silent alarm had just gone off.

Bob arrived perplexed and slightly annoyed.

"Bob," Sid said, "this is John Peters. He's in from out of town. We want to ask you a few questions."

"Glad to meet you," he said.

"Bob, I'll give it to you straight. You've been followed. Did y' know that?"

"No, I didn't. What the…"

"You were tailed when you left the office a little while ago. Here's a picture of who followed you. We just snapped it a few days ago. Do y' know him?"

"No, I don't believe I do. I've never seen this man before in my life. Why is he fuckin' tailing me?"

"That's what John and I would like to know. Are you sure?"

"I told you, no, I don't fuckin' know him."

"Have you ever been to Cleveland, Bob, or anywhere near there?"

"Hell no. I was born and raised in New Orleans, never even left it for a vacation."

"Christ, John. There must be a reason…"

"There is Sid. There is a reason for this whole mess. All we have to do is find it."

"Well, what am I supposed to do? Stop working and just stay home? I have to earn for my family just like you have to earn."

"First, can your wife and children pack up and go stay with a relative out of town?"

"Yes…they can."

"Do it now. Get 'em away before it gets dark. I'm getting two other men to stay with you. They'll be with you at all times. When you come home, stay there. The two men will be with you but it won't be obvious to any outsiders. I don't want you to go anywhere yourself. Do you follow me so far?"

"Yeah, I do. How long will this go on for? Do you know?"

"I don't know Bob. We have to find out if he's really after you. But don't worry. We'll be with you at all times. You may not see us at times, but we'll be there. Just follow orders. It could save your life."

We kept a constant vigil on "Fat Boy" never letting him out of our sight. He had dropped his pal, and was by himself now. He stuck to Bob like glue and didn't seem to know we were keeping him under observation as well.

For the next week the routine never varied. He would follow Bob and park near his home. He would wait until the early hours of the morning, four or five AM, and then finally drive away. We would follow and stay with him until we made sure he was in his bed, tucked in so to speak.

Our tailing was over until the next day when Bob would leave the office again. Once more, "Fat Boy" followed him. He was cool and patient. It didn't seem like his first job and I was curious to know why…

Finally, we had our answer. It came from the New York office, addressed to me. Sid was asleep at the time at the house we were using to watch the "Fat Boy"...something we weren't getting much of these days.

"Wake up," I said as I shook him. "We finally have our answer. Listen...it seems that our man is a little off his rocker. He isn't a union man at all, but he has a bitch against unions, any unions. It's just your misfortune that he picked on you this time...

"Apparently, he had a shop in Cleveland, almost seven years ago. He was involved in a union fight, not even our union, and he fought with all he had. Y' know the whole scenario. He met with a few accidents, but wouldn't give in. He had plenty of money, so the fight lasted a long time. He was driving the unions crazy, costing them a fortune, so they had to do something. It looks like they tried to blow him up in his car, but instead they got his wife and daughter. They were both found burned to death.

"Harsh, I know, Sid. I don't condone them. Anyway he went crazy. He went gunning for the union president,—killed him too...but he beat the rap and got put in an insane asylum instead. About three years ago, he got out. Now he wants to avenge his wife and daughter. I guess, any union will do.

"What New York thinks is that he must take several trips a year. Whenever he returns to Cleveland, another unsolved murder of some union member pops up. Sid, you know how we always keep things to ourselves, even here. When something happens, we keep it quiet and take care of it ourselves...so do the other unions. The result is that no one knew about the unsolved murders except each individual union.

"New York has gone to a lot of trouble to get this information. They made a deal with another union to work on this...unheard of, I know. But it's in your lap now, Sid."

"Let's go over and talk to Bob, John."

We found him in the office, and he was a sorry sight. His nerves were frayed and he looked tired and worn. He sailed into us when he saw us.

"I can't fuckin' take this much longer. I'm at the end of my rope...I'm a wreck and I need sleep. You've gotta fuckin' do something..."

I looked at him with disgust. What a cherry. But here goes the bullshit.

"Your worries are just about over," I told him. "In order to find out if this guy was really our man, we had to dangle you. I'm sure you knew that and everything was voluntary on your part. You had a lot of balls to sacrifice these past few days for the union.

"Now, tonight you go home. Stick to the same routine, only at three AM, you go outta your house, hop in your car, and drive off...you won't be in any danger. If he's watching, you'll take him by surprise.

"Get onto Canal Street and drive down it slow and easy. Canal runs into a dead end at the cemetery. You have to make a sharp right turn and then a left to get back onto Canal. Do y' know where it is?..."

"Yeah, I know where it is..."

"Good. Except I don't want you to go back on Canal. Approach the dead end slowly and just before you make the right turn, hit the gas hard and keep going straight. Go past the cemetery and get the hell outta there as fast as you can. Keep going until you reach home...do you understand?"

"You know something," Bob said. "Why should I risk my balls for you? You had your damn nerve using me like that!"

"Look, you bastard, you would've been a fuckin' corpse two weeks ago if me and Sid hadn't spotted this guy to begin with. We guarded you at all times until we were sure, until we found out the reason why. So keep your fuckin' mouth shut and follow my damn orders."

After he left, I turned to Sid.

"He ain't got any balls. Not even for excitement. I don't know how he got into the union, he's the first one I've met that you can't depend on...you're aware that he'll have to go, aren't you?"

"Yeah." He said wearily. "I know."

I drove the Buick and parked it a block behind Bob's house and we waited. Bob's car pulled up and he and his bodyguards entered the house. Within thirty seconds, the "Fat Boy" pulled up. The night dragged on and I must've dozed off for I felt Sid nudging me. I quickly woke up. I looked at my watch it said, ten to three.

"Anything go wrong?" I asked.

"No. Nothing is happening yet. "Fat Boy" doesn't even know we're here. However, it looks like he has a long object in his car. Maybe a rifle?"

At three o'clock on the dot the front door opened. Bob quickly stepped outside, got into his car and drove off like he was being chased by cops or something.

"Bastard," I said. "We told him to fuckin' take it slow and easy. If he fuck's this up, I'll kill him myself."

The "Fat Boy" started his car and followed Bob. We joined the procession as it went down Canal Street. There was still a little night traffic, just enough to prevent our man from doing anything. We were nearing the end of the street when I saw "Fat Boy" begin to roll down the window on his right side, keeping one hand on his steering wheel and the other steadying his rifle.

"He's loaded. He's gonna shoot!" I shouted.

"That's it, John." Sid took out his forty-five and began to take aim.

"Don't miss damn it. We have only a slight chance here."

"I won't, Tom. This guy is responsible for the death of two of my crew. I have nothing but hate for him."

Bob's car shot ahead in a burst of speed suddenly, taking the corner on two wheels and disappeared. Our man tried to take the corner a moment later. I came right up beside him, taking the corner at the same time, while both cars' wheels squealed and screamed as they straightened out, side by side.

With one eye on the road and one eye on him, I saw him make a sudden turn with his head and look directly at us. In an instant, I heard a gun go off...the bullets flew smack into his face and embedded themselves there. He raised his hands to his face, the rifle still clutched in one hand, as the steering wheel spun freely and the car swerved and crashed.

I hit the gas and was out of there. I dropped Sid off at a local diner. I checked out of my hotel and grabbed the first plane. Good times in New Orleans would have to wait.

CHAPTER 20

▼

TIME BOMB

Chapter Twenty

I returned to New York and was given a new shop to organize. Half of the workers joined with us, and we threw up a picket line. Then everything went sour.

Another union approached the boss with a sweetheart contract and he accepted. This was one beef that we had to settle fast. We were paying the men to help them meet ends and were losing a small fortune. The police made it known they would not tolerate any violence and helped the opposing union's workers pass right through our line. The scabs kept working and collecting their pay checks, and our line became useless.

John lost his temper.

"Tom, what the fuck are you gonna do with this shop? This has been dragging out too long. Something has to be fuckin' done and done fast. This line is costing us a small fortune. Have you lost your balls?"

"You told me, John, to go easy. No rough stuff. Be nice, Tom. How do you expect me to sign up a shop with those kind of orders? If you're so worried about losing money, then give the whole shop to the other union and shake it off the books. I don't give a damn."

John raised himself from his chair and pounded his fist on the top of his desk.

"You fuckin' stand there and ask me why we can't afford to lose one lousy shop with seventy employees? Have you learned nothing in all these years?"

He leaned forward and slammed his fist on the desk again. He raised his voice again and shouted, "I'll fuckin' tell you why. You lose one shop, you lose them all. Pretty soon, every shop we try to take after that will fight us. They won't think we're the strongest. All the other unions will have a fuckin' edge on us. They'll see we're weakening. We don't give up without a fight, you get it?

"So here's what I've decided," he said sternly. "If we can't have this shop, no one will. I'll have the fuckin' whole place destroyed and put out of business. Then no one will fuckin' 'cross us."

"You're kidding. You're serious, John?"

"If you can't do it, I'll find someone who will...you tell the workers who joined us they have nothing to fear. We can place them in other shops. But I want that shop destroyed. And here's how it's going to be done."

He opened his desk draw and took out a package.

"This beauty, is a time bomb. It's simple and easy to operate. I want you to do it and no one else. You set the time, you press this little button, and you walk away. Then, it goes off at the time you set. Like I said, it's simple."

"Y' know, I never saw you use one of these things. I'm just a little surprised. It may be simple to you, but are you sure, John, that it won't go off accidentally?"

"Never be surprised. Not in our business. I wasn't born yesterday, y' know. When I make one of these babies, my guarantee goes along with it. I can't afford to make even the slightest mistake. No, there isn't a chance of it going off before schedule, believe me. But don't throw it around. I'd handle it with kid gloves."

I began to examine the bomb and was a bit amazed.

"You made this? There really is no end to your capabilities, is there?"

"It's a little hobby of mine, Tom. Besides, this way, it can't be traced. Don't ever buy one from someone. If he talks, you're finished. This is the best way. Now go do your fuckin' job."

The night was black and moonless when I parked my car near the factory. I picked this Saturday because there was no night shift on the weekend. The place would be vacant except for the old watchman.

He had four clocks spread throughout the shop to check. They were alarms connected to police headquarters. One was in the cellar, one was in a different store room, the third was in the machine room, and the fourth was in the front of the building. On the hour he had to enter each room and check the clock alarms, insert a key into each clock which then registered at headquarters. If too much time elapsed between the clocks' coordination, the police would drive to the shop and check for themselves.

This was the only thing I had to watch out for. The watchman could take anywhere between ten and twenty minutes to finish his check.

At ten minutes to eleven, I walked quietly through the alley towards the rear of the shop. The large wooden door had an old fashioned, heavy padlock. I took a small bottle out of my pocket and poured the liquid onto the lock. The tough, rusty metal burned easily. It fizzled as the acid did its trick in about fifteen minutes. I had hoped it would go faster, so I waited an extra five minutes for the watchman to clear the machine room.

I was in dimly lit surroundings but I knew it was the machine room. I closed my eyes and tried to identify all the sounds in the shop to get my bearings. I knew the watchman sat in the office at night. I snuck in there, muffled sneakers and all, and there he was, dozing already. It was easy to creep up behind him and knock him unconscious.

He grunted as his face hit the table. I turned him over quickly and felt the beat of his heart. I couldn't leave him there. The place was going to blow. So I dragged his body out to the back alley, then raced back inside. I was hoping he would think he was luckily thrown out of the shop when it blew sky-high.

I lifted my little, fragile, package and stepped toward's the center of the room. I picked the machine out and strapped the bomb to its legs, then set it carefully, timing it to go off in fifteen minutes. Everything had gone along perfectly. Excellent! All I had to do was press the button and leave.

By the time I had reached my car, eight minutes had elapsed. I was six blocks from the shop when I heard the explosion. I turned to look in the shop's direction and it was the Fourth of July against the pitch black sky. I stepped on the gas and headed to New Jersey where my alibi waited.

It was Monday and I had just parked my car in front of my apartment house. Two men were waiting for me and they smelled of cops. One of them shoved a badge in front of my face.

"You, Thomas Furcco?"

"Yeah, that's me. Can I help you Gentlemen?"

"Okay. Let's go."

"Go where?"

"Shut the hell up and let's go."

"Are you gonna tell me what the hell this is about? Because I'm not going anywhere until you tell me."

"Are you in charge of the strike at Manning's?"

"Y' know I am. So what?"

"Oh shit, Tom. Are you gonna tell us you don't know anything about the plant going up on Saturday night?"

"Yeah, I do. It was in the papers."

"Oh, I see. Whattaya think we're stupid?"

"You think I had something to do with this?"

"Yes, we do. Come on downtown. We need to talk to you."

"Y' know, I have a very good friend in Southern New Jersey. I've been down there since Friday night and just came back. You can check if you want...I don't see you arresting me...so this is fuckin' settled..."

"Y' know, Tom. You better take a good word of advice."

The two detectives glanced around the lot, then at each other. The next thing I knew I was bowled over, then kicked a few times. One of them picked me up like a sack of potatoes and threw me horizontally across the sidewalk like I was a piece of shit.

It was futile, I knew. I just had to let them take it out on me. But I gritted inside. I would get even. They finished leaning closest to my bruised face so I could taste their bad breath.

"Tom, we're warning you. You just missed a step here, and fell right, having too much trouble with strikes in this town. This bombing is gonna create hell for everyone now. If I find out that you or any of your crew was involved in this, I'll hang you by your balls myself...understand? I'll really throw the book at you..."

They took off quickly as another car was just pulling in.

When I finally made it to my apartment, I called John. He agreed to meet me at his private club.

"I was going to send someone to the station. I heard they were gonna try to pinch you."

"They can't. They don't have any witnesses, and I have an alibi. No one was hurt, so they can't go hunting for a murderer. I was smart. I knocked out the watchman and pulled him out. It's just a plain rubble of a shop that's gone. That's all."

"They shouldn't have roughed you up. Don't do anything foolish. Remember, think clearly. Don't go planning to cut them up or something...I think we'll just have our lawyer complain to their chief. Threaten to release it to the papers. It will make great press. Union leader, beaten up because other union resorts to bombing. Let me take care of this."

We whispered this conversation behind closed doors. It was a private club, and you couldn't get in to begin with unless you were a member or connected. The drinks were good at least. I was starting to cop a buzz when I finally hit the highway to go home. I should have followed John's advice. He wanted to call a cab for me.

I kept the speedometer at thirty-five, cruising along the deserted road. I was trying to feel good again, singing to the radio when I glanced in the rear view mirror. I spotted a pair of headlights behind me about a hundred yards away. As it neared my car, the driver pulled to the left as if to pass me, but he didn't pass. He began to slow down.

My head cleared in a second as I automatically pressed down on the accelerator. My car bolted ahead as I picked up speed and pulled away from him.

I had caught him by surprise, but very quickly he picked up speed and came after me.

I hit a cut-off at seventy-five miles an hour and I heard my own tires start to scream. I tried to straighten out my car to keep it on the road as my eyes darted to my mirror. He was still behind me. Then, I heard the sound of breaking glass. I lunged forward over my wheel...my rear window had been shot away...

My heart skipped a beat. The speed indicator read a dangerous ninety miles an hour and the distance that separated us was comparatively small. I just knew he was going to stay with me and he wasn't going to take no for an answer...

I tried to get my bearings. I suddenly remembered the layout of the road before me and I knew I would be in trouble. Two miles ahead was a curve, then a straight stretch of road for about a mile. At the end of that stretch was going to be my problem. It was a circle. I knew I could not make that circle at this speed...I would be splattered all over the landscape. How convenient. My assailant would accomplish what he had to do and his hands would be clean. I had to think quickly.

I reached the curve and followed the straight road. Then I turned the wheel slightly to get the car driving on the road's shoulder while braking and turning off my lights at the same time. I felt the car slow down and spun it behind an empty gas station. I only had enough time to hug the ground when the other car's headlights poked through the dark.

He bulldozed on ahead. I heard his tires screeching, but no sounds of a crash. He had evidently made the circle. It seemed like an eternity before I spotted his headlights again. My heart pounded as the car slowed down and passed me. As it did, I could see three men in the car, and I recognized one of them...it was Dave, from the other union. They didn't spot me and I lay there tense, sweating for at least half an hour. They didn't double back.

Finally, I was sitting behind my wheel, trying to breathe again. So it was the other union who was trying to gun me down and Dave who wanted my hide. Just because they almost had that shop signed up before it was blasted. Why does he think it was me? Damn fuckin' cops. They must have been dropping hints to him. Now I'm unfinished business. Great. Well, can't go home now. They'll be waiting for me. Have to dump the car too. Have to get out of town. Have to, have to, have to...

I drove towards home with my eye over my shoulder the whole time. I parked about half a mile from my house. I walked to my house slowly through the back streets, pausing often. Then I waited a full hour watching to see if anyone was around. I decided to take the chance and bolted to my door. I had to grab my gun, knife, and cash, all hidden carefully. I took no chances. The phone rang but I didn't answer.

I was out of there as if set on fire. I walked another mile before hailing a cab and took it to a hotel on the other side of the Hudson. There was a used car lot near where I decided to stay for the night. In the morning, I would have a new car to get out of town with.

CHAPTER 21

▼

MESSING UP

Chapter Twenty-One

For three days I stayed low and out of circulation. Then I started staking out Dave's house. I hated him. This job would go easier with all the hate inside of me. On the third day, I finally spotted him…the disgusting little piece of shit. I quickly followed him and crept up behind him and jabbed my gun into his back.

"Into the alley," I commanded him as I roughly pushed him towards the narrow, back street. When we got in the alley, he turned around and looked into my face.

"Well, if it isn't my old friend, Tom. We were wondering what happened to you…haven't seen ya in a while? So what's the fuckin' problem?"

"What's the problem, you bastard? Whattaya think, you can try to gun me down and I'll just forget about it Dave?

"You fucked up, Dave," I angrily threw my breath and spit into his face. "I'm surprised, Dave, you were very careless…you let me see your face, and I don't forget. So, you wanna play rough?"

I raised my hand and hit him on the side of the head with my gun. As his body started to crumble to the ground, I kicked him in the ribs…his body rose with the kick then fell to the ground like a ship tossed by a wave at sea. When he started to get up, I placed another well aimed kick and he fell back to the ground landing in a pile of trash.

"That's where you belong, Dave. But, I'm not finished yet. You wanted to kill me and think you're gonna just waltz around?"

I grabbed him by the lapels and jerked him to his feet. I lost control and kept hitting him while I propped him against the wall.

"Stay just the way you are, don't move or turn around…if you do, I'll shoot," said a loud, forceful voice out of no where, behind me.

I stood perfectly still.

"Drop the gun nice and easy and put your hands in the air, high, where I can see 'em," he continued.

I tossed my gun aside and let go of Dave's body as I raised my hands high in the air.

"That's right, nice and easy. Now put your hands against the wall and spread your legs."

I did what I was told. He pulled at my arms and slapped on handcuffs. Then he patted me down and shoved me away from Dave. As I turned around my eyes only saw the big, thirty-eight in the hands of a cop who was just as big. Two other policemen suddenly huddled near Dave's body.

Great Tom. Just great. Boy did I fuck up. Dumb, dumb, dumb. I should've controlled my anger. I should've planned this better. Taken him to someplace deserted. No, I had to do this here...boy, this is nice. Caught red-handed, the body in front of me, an unregistered gun and no brains. Never get caught, right, Tom? Boy what a damn mess...

I was hustled roughly out of the alley and put in a patrol car. An ambulance had arrived and they carried Dave out on a stretcher. Within minutes, we landed at police headquarters. My favorite captain. He's going to love putting me away on this one.

"Well, well, well...we finally have our boy, don't we?" He glanced at the patrolman's notes. "Assault with a deadly weapon, assault with intent to kill, assault and battery, possession of a concealed weapon, no gun permit...oh, yes!...If he dies, MURDER!...Conspiracy to commit murder!...Yeah, we finally have you and I'm going to throw the book at you."

"I want my phone call." I said angrily.

"You hear that, everybody?" The captain laughed and all the other cops joined in. "He wants his phone call. What the fuck are you gonna do if I don't let you?" he sneered. "Absolutely nothing. Take this piece of shit away. Book him, finger print him, lock him up."

After they took my picture and finger printed me, they inspected my clothes and body again. They took my shoe laces and belt, matches, keys, cash.

"One hundred in small bills, huh, Tom? We'll just hold onto this ourselves, for our little widows' fund. You don't mind, do you? Here, you can have your cigarettes. Too bad about no light...and, let's not forget to give him his lousy phone call. Then it's off to a nice cell for you. We've picked out a beaut. No bathroom, sorry. Yep, you're going to be here for a while."

I called John for his help. Of course, we had a lawyer, but this wasn't union business. It was personal and I got caught. I could almost feel John's agitation and disappointment. He doubted I could even make bail. And God forbid, Dave died. I would be indicted for murder, not manslaughter, and would get life or the gas chamber.

I was led down a flight of stairs, to the dungeons, as they were nick-named, past two securely locked doors and several more cops on guard, and then thrown in a cell. The gate slammed shut and I could have screamed. There was no window, nothing, no way out at all and I sat there trying to calculate how far I could get if I wrestled one of the guards down. Stupid, stupid, Tom. A trapped little animal.

And I rotted there, for four lousy days. Then, suddenly, John's lawyer showed up and I was released. Dave had taken a turn for the better and my bail was paid, a handsome five thousand. They didn't think he would press charges, but I had to report to a probation office once a week, and to John, right now, who was sitting in the car when I stepped out of the police station.

"You're hearing won't be coming up for a while…" John said shaking his head inside the car.

"Why couldn't you get me out on bail sooner?"

"I can't fuckin' believe you lost it," John shouted. "Don't you fuckin' understand that you could have been indicted for murder if that bastard had died? And the captain; that captain has a bug up his ass for you…"

"He won't die. I didn't hit him that hard," I replied like an asshole.

"Don't try to con me, Tom! Why weren't you more careful? I mean you beat some bastard up and it's just minutes from police headquarters? What the fuck happened to your brain? And it's the other union you went after. So, now you've implicated us in all of this. Are you fuckin' crazy? Do you know how hot it is with this bombing and everything? Why, Tom? Now we have a big problem, not just with the police but with fuckin' Dave's union also."

"John, I just got hot under the collar and went off. They went after me after I left the club. Dave came close to killing me. I was lucky, I escaped. Go look at my car. It's parked about half a mile away from my house. The whole rear window is shot out. I was only taking care of the bastard. What was I supposed to do? Shake the bastard's hand and ask him for a drink for trying to run me off the road and shoot at me?"

"So he thinks you were involved with the bombing, then…you know, Tom, why didn't you just call me after this happened? You didn't think this through, just lost your damn hot temper and now look at the hole you've put yourself in…the only reason I'm helping you is because I'm your friend…

"So, here's what I'm gonna do. I want you outta town until this thing is settled. Except for your weekly visits to the probation officer, I want you to steer clear of this place. Just go and keep outta sight….did the cops try to question you about the bombing?"

"I didn't say anything. I took the fifth."

"Good. Just don't talk to 'em at all tell 'em to contact your attorney. You're gonna have to watch your back and be extra careful and alert...and Tom, y' know we can't have any contact together now, not for a long time...I won't care if you forfeit the bail and take off...y' know?" he said shrewdly.

"Tom, you and I know, you're sitting on a time bomb right now. If Dave decides not to press charges, it won't be because he loves you. He'll still be gunning for revenge, and you can bet he won't make the same mistake you made..."

"John, I'm not running anywhere, not from anyone or anything. If they find me I'll deal with it, but I'm not running."

"God damn it Tom, don't make this personal...I can't use you until this whole mess is over. You're too hot right now and you're gonna find your brains in the street, but go ahead, get your head busted open, but stop coming to me for help."

"Okay, John. If you think it's the best thing, I'll go along with you and disappear. I'll just drop outta sight. If you need me, just give me the word."

He handed me my probation papers, and a thick envelope with cash, and said nothing else for the rest of the car ride.

At the train station, Joan's face came to mind. I wondered about her, and decided to give her another call.

Chapter 22

▼

MY PROPOSAL

Chapter Twenty-Two

I made a date with Joan and found myself returning to the town I despised. It wasn't too big and it wasn't too small. I had managed to disappear there once without a trace, so it seemed as good a place as ever for now. It wouldn't be too easy for someone to look for you.

Well, this time Joan showed up. It had been about a year since I seen her. I recognized her instantly when she walked in. Her beauty was still enchanting and nothing seemed to have changed. I stood up gallantly.

"How are you, Joan?" I asked her as she sat down in the booth.

"I'm fine. And you? It's nice to see you again. Where've you been?…"

"I wasn't sure you'd show up. You didn't the last time…"

"I'm sorry. I didn't have your number to call…to postpone our date…I really am so sorry…I didn't think we would ever see each other again…I've been so angry with myself about that…but, you could've called too?"

"I did, last year…your husband answered the phone, so there wasn't much in talking to him…I just left town instead…well, at least I called and found you this time."

"Where have you been?"

"Virginia Beach. I stayed there for a while, just taking it easy…y' know, I can't stay in this town for long…there are too many unhappy memories…my dead wife…y' know…I just arrived in town and felt I had to get in touch with you…you've been on my mind for some time now."

Joan smiled.

"You should've called sooner. I wondered what happened to you."

"Joan, it's been almost a year since I last saw you and time hasn't changed you at all. In fact, you're even more beautiful…why is that?" I said gently taking her slender hand in mine.

"Now, Tom…you're gonna make me blush…it has been a long time and I've thought of you many times also…I was so surprised when I didn't see you around the tavern. Even some of your friends didn't know your whereabouts…you could've written or called…but, I'm glad you're here now."

"Joan, I haven't had ties on me for so long. Guess it's hard to teach an old dog new tricks. I just come and go as I please. And, as long as the kids are taken care of, I'm satisfied. Besides, I hate this place. I probably won't be in town for long, so let's make the best of it now. Let me make this up to you. I wanna spend every single day with you now. Let's get to know each other."

"Oh?...Okay. I wouldn't mind that. Is that why you came back? Just to be with me?"

"I like you a lot Joan...yes, that's why. I just wanted to see you again...are you still married?"

"I guess you could say that. I really should investigate a divorce...but, I don't know...I've got an idea...why don't we spend time with each other and just not talk about it?"

"Okay. But you know it's gonna come up...maybe I can change your mind?"

We ordered drinks and talked and danced all night. We only had eyes for each other. It felt like we were the only two people there and time rushed by us and stood still at the same time. She relaxed me. This wasn't a bump and grind number. She was different. She was beautiful. She was soft, gentle, intelligent, compassionate, and in her deep, brown eyes I saw all time stop and only love. Through her deep, brown eyes I saw only the tenderest of futures, only the best of times yet to come.

Did she feel the same? Then why were we together? Was it that I changed or that the rough union organizer exterior melted away whenever I was with her? I strangely behaved like a gentleman around her. I couldn't even bring myself to swear in her company. My favorite and special antic with her was to make sure she never lit her own cigarette. And I took special pains to protect her from everybody and everything.

I sent her flowers and perfumes, and bought her jewelry and silks, all kinds of presents...I rented a house for us both, and we spent our special, private times there, day and night. We went everywhere together, all over the place...breakfasts, lunches, dinners, dancing, nights together, days together. You would've thought we were newlyweds. Yes, this was love for me...

"Tom, can I ask you a personal question? Y' know, I usually don't pry, but, are you wealthy? I mean, you spend all this money on me and I never see you work...I'm just curious, where do you go out of town once a week?"

"Joan, I've always made top money...much better than most. I guess you could say I've saved plenty. I go to see my boys once a week outta town."

"But, you're not a millionaire. How large could your savings be? What will happen when it runs out?"

"Look, hon. Let's drop it. When the right time comes, sometime soon, I'll tell you everything about me. But until then, you'll have to trust me...okay, beautiful?..."

"I'm sorry...course, you're right. I'm just gonna spoil the day with all these questions. I trust you, Tom. I always feel safe with you. I just relax with you and never seem to worry about anything. You are special to me, y' know that. I feel wonderful...no, there's not a word that can describe how happy I am to be with you."

"I feel the same way, Joan. I love you, y' know that...I haven't felt this way since my first marriage...I wanna marry you, Joan...for life..."

Time froze again. You could only hear the soft breeze and the warmth of the sunshine glittering on the lake. I took out a small ring box. She just stared at it, and then tears slipped down her beautiful, porcelain face.

"Oh, Tom. Y' know, y' know. I love you so, but I can't. I just can't...I have a husband, and you know that even though I don't live with him much and don't love him at all, I just can't marry you."

"So, all this time we've spent together, means nothing now? Honey, I don't think you know what love is. One of these days, you're gonna wake up and find out you are truly in love with me, but I may be gone, permanently."

"But, Tom. You're different from anyone I ever known. You're exciting, suave, personable, kind...I just wanna be sure it's love, not just fascination...I've already been burned once."

"Alright...so I'll wait...but time stops for no one...y' know the old saying. So we'll wait but you have to get to the bottom of your feelings and stop feeling so confused...I've been burned too, only differently, through death...so I know what it's like. Just don't take too long, Joan...please honey, don't take too long..."

"I'm sorry, Tom. Let's forget about this right now or I'm going to ruin the day for us...and, I will...get back to you and give you an answer. Just give me a little more time...please..."

Dave dropped the charges against me. The mess had passed. But John said I got blackmailed. Someone sure wanted to make some of those charges stick. One thousand dollars I had to pay. John never said to who, but told me I was lucky. He didn't think Dave would just go away though. Dave wanted me out, so he could get a second chance at my ass. The word was getting around that he wanted revenge and he wanted it bad.

John told me to take a couple of weeks off and stay far, far away from Dave in particular.

"Go get married for Christ's sake, if you're so head over heels about this girl...but get lost. We're union men and we're not suppose to get sentimental...good luck..."

I was free and clear finally. Should I break the union code of not telling our women about our business, should I tell Joan? Was she ever going to marry me? Maybe I should settle down. Maybe I should get out. Well, there was only one way to find out if she loved me. I was going to break a major rule of the union, I was going to tell her, tell her about the jam with Dave...see if it scared her off or brought her to my side.

"Joan, I think it's about time you and I had that little talk we mentioned some time back. You wanted to know more about me, what kind of work I did..."

Joan sat down, always so beautiful.

"Yes, Tom. What do you want to say? You're going to tell me about how you stole candy as a child from the local candy store?"

"I don't know how you're gonna take this. I work for a union, the biggest, most powerful, and strongest union on the east coast. I'm a union organizer. A top boss."

"Tom? I don't know anything about unions. Are you trying to tell me something bad?"

"Well, sometimes we have to use dirty and forceful tactics to accomplish our aims. Those trips that I've been taking once a week were really about this mess I got myself in. I wasn't goin' to see my sons, I was reporting to a probation office..."

Joan's face paled and she became very nervous.

"What, Tom? This is terrible. But, what kind of person are you?"

"Honey, hear me out. It's not as bad as you think. This guy's a gangster. He tried to kill me because I ran a union strike against his union. He almost killed me. I lost it and beat him up. So I got arrested. He didn't exactly die. Anyways, the charges were dropped, and it's all over now...I just wanted you to know the truth...no lies, not between us..."

Joan looked at me in horror with her mouth half opened. It was a few moments before she regained her composure and spoke to me.

"I, I...Is that what you've been doing?...That's where you get your money?...What kind of man am I going with?"

"What do you mean, what kind of man are you goin' with?...The man you fell in love with...I'm still the same. This is my job, and you may not like to hear this, but I like my work. The union is special, not just for all the workers, but it's filled with action, power, excitement...my work is for the future, and that's what I like. Here, you're calling me a gangster when you don't even know the full story. You don't even know what a union is. And then you condemn me for harming someone when you don't even know the whole circumstances."

"I don't know, Tom. I don't know very much about unions, but this seems so, so illegal. How could you? How could you be involved in something so vicious?"

"Honey, I wanna marry you. If I thought I could have you, I would get out, give it up entirely. That's my offer. That's how much you mean to me. I'd do anything you ask, just give me a chance. Tell me you love me. We can have a home, a clean, decent life. Just say the word."

"Oh, Tom. Why did you have to tell me?...I don't know what I want...I want you to get out of this business. I wanna tell you I love you but I'm so confused now."

"But, Joan. I don't wanna have to keep fighting you, just to have you. I need you to want me as much as I want you. If you told me right now you loved me, we could be married tonight. But I can't go on this way. I must either have you or stay away from you completely. It's because of what I do, isn't it?"

"No, Tom. It isn't that. You're sweet and kind to me. I get butterflies in my stomach when I'm with you. I feel like a teenager sometimes. But, is it you I love or is it because you treat me as if I were so rare and special? Because you're different from any other person that I have ever known...y' know I don't love my husband. In fact, since I met you I really despise him now...I would leave him in an instant and go with you, but I have to be sure. I messed up my life with one bad marriage. I don't want to make the same mistake again. And ruin your life in the bargain? Maybe you should go away for a while and let me think..."

"Well, which is it, Joan? If I leave I'll return to the union. If I leave the union, it'll be so as not to lose you. You don't want me to stay here...you don't want me to return to the union. If you want me bad enough, marry me, Joan. If I can't have you, I'll return to the union and I'll be even more ruthless. I'll take it all out on someone else."

"No," she yelled.

"All you have to do is leave your God damn, sick husband who you don't love anyway! You could get a divorce. I don't want to force you into this, but we could get married, live anywhere you want, I could start a small business. I can't stand this merry-go-round. Make up your mind…"

"Oh!" She stood up and almost in tears, shouted, "Do whatever you want and leave me alone," and she stormed out of the room.

CHAPTER 23

▼

ONE LAST JOB

Chapter Twenty-Three

"Cozy," I said.

"Yeah, this is kind of nice. I like it myself. Well, make yourself at home. There's beer in the refrigerator. You should just rest up a little after driving. I'll go get the bags."

Pete Ferretti left to unload the car. I propped my feet up and tried to relax.

I had accepted another union assignment thanks to Joan. Why did I? Would this be my last union job? I didn't know. Funny how a woman can drive you over the edge a little. I tried so hard to straighten things out with her, but it was futile. I should've never broken that first union rule. She kept telling me to go away for a few days and let her think, so went away I did.

Well it was cozy at least. It was the kind of cabin I should have taken Joan to. We could've spent a grand week or two here. Instead, I had driven to Connecticut to spend the week with a wise guy chasing down God only knows who. How ironic.

"You should take it easy today, Tom...you need anything else? The bar and restaurant are right down by the corner. You can even walk there."

"No, I'm fine. When you getting back?"

"I'll see you eight-thirty or nine tonight...OK? We'll take your car. Out of state plates make you a tourist—less noticeable. Tonight we stake out Frank...Frank Tergandi, does that ring a bell?"

"No. Pete, I remember faces, not names."

"Over there, about ten, fifteen minutes, there's a clearing and an abandoned house. Pretty deserted. We might need that area. Check it out if you can. I'll do the driving tonight."

Great. Pete had been planning. That was good. We didn't need another bad deal like the last one. I grabbed a bite to eat and a few drinks at the hotel down the street, then took a little drive to get acquainted with the area.

It was unbelievably quiet, countrified, peaceful. I found the deserted house that Pete had talked about. It was deserted alright. The doors and windows were heavily boarded up and the grass was high with no one around. I drove further down the road and found the clearing towards the trees in front of me.

You could hardly walk through it, the weeds and overgrowth were so thick. Yeah, this would be a good spot, deserted, hidden. It could come in handy. The only thing I had to do was rehearse going there so that I'd know the terrain like the back of my hand. That could wait until tomorrow.

Pete picked me up at nine and we bolted to the expressway.

"How come no traffic?"

I was surprised. We hadn't passed a car yet in spite of the fact that it was a beautiful, balmy night.

"I don't know, Tom. It seems to slow down a lot about this time of night."

We turned at a cut off, drove a little more through the city, and finally parked the car across from an enormous house. I looked at the house and whistled.

"What a joint! What did they do? Stud it with diamonds?"

"Worth around a hundred grand."

"Hold on, Pete. I've taken on lots of jobs with all classes of people, but I never had a target from a mansion like this. So who is he?"

"He's the boss of a union we want to move in on…a real big boss. There are a few shops we're trying to organize and he's stopping our every move. Four of my crew are mysteriously missing. I blame him, but haven't a shred of proof."

"Pete he's a fuckin' boss, are you out of your fuckin' mind? We'll start a bloodbath of a war. You think if he meets up with an accident, he'll change his mind and just let you walk into those shops?"

"I don't think it will be that easy.

"But maybe when he realizes that we're strong enough to fight him…if he knows we mean business, he might scare a little…well, it just has to be done."

"Does he have any favorite habits or hangouts?"

"That's part of the problem. He doesn't. We'll have to stick to him until the right opportunity presents itself."

We waited for a hour or two, but Tergandi didn't appear, so we headed back to my cabin.

"Get a good night's sleep, Tom. We can try again tomorrow. If necessary, we can sleep in the car and wait, but not your first night. Rest up. Pick you up in the morning, about eight AM?"

I slept soundly. An assignment did that for me. I always liked that mix of excitement, power, and adrenaline. And the fresh, country, night air acted like a sedative. Everything felt good. Except for Joan. Except for Joan's episode and indecisiveness, I could've been somewhere else, with her in my arms…

I awoke to a beautiful morning. The sun was a ball of fire coming up over the hills. Birds sung everywhere, and trees rustled. I almost wished I was on vacation. Joan and I could've booked this little cabin. We could've had a nice time. It could've been a quiet honeymoon even…

A tall man emerged from the mansion. Pete and I had parked the car as inconspicuously as possible.

"That's him," Pete whispered and poked at me. "That's Frank Tergandi."

He was big, about six foot three or four, with a build to match. At least two hundred and twenty pounds covered his solid frame, with brown wavy hair. He looked like a boss.

"Is he married, Pete?"

"Yeah, with two kids. Rumor has it he married the missus for her money."

"How old is he?"

"Forty-three, I think. And don't let that wavy, hair and good looks fool you. He's rough and tough. Came to this area about five years ago as a delegate. He was ambitious, ruthless and cruel then. He didn't get where he's today by being nice, if you know what I mean. He's been boss for three years now and has become so powerful that it's impossible to surpass him."

While Pete was talking, a car pulled into the driveway with two men in it. One got out and held the door open for Tergandi who proceeded to get into the back seat. I turned to Pete for an explanation.

"The Gold Dust twins," he said. "Bodyguards."

"But, Pete, they all practically look alike from this distance…how interesting…"

"They never leave his side for a minute for as long as he's out of the house. He has another one in the house acting like a sort of butler. You see what we are up against? There's no way to get near him because he's rarely alone. And then, they like to trade places…neat, huh?…Yeah, our guy's very slippery."

"Well, you know that old saying, Pete. The bigger they are, the harder they fall."

"Well, we're off and running now. Today is collection day. You'll see. We'll tail 'em all day and nothing will come of it. They'll drive to a factory, two of 'em will get out, and one will stay with the car, then ten or fifteen minutes later they'll leave and head for another plant. After a few stops, you won't know which one is which."

"How come the boss collects the dues? They got a different system?..."

"What he's collecting isn't dues...it's payoffs. All in cash. The shop owners pay him personally. He wants it that way...no records, no witnesses, nothing to prove he received them."

"Are you kidding, Pete? Protection in this day and age?"

"It isn't called protection, Tom. The word is assessments. You should know about them. You collected enough of 'em yourself."

"Yeah, but our money was automatically taken out of the workers' paychecks."

"Well, Tergandi has another way of handling this. The owners pay, the payoff is quite high, all in cash, and it goes directly into Tergandi's own pocket. Nice, huh?..."

The day went pretty much the way Pete said it would. The only thing we noticed was that after Tergandi visited a shop, they would all stop off and have a drink. His consumption was enormous. He liked to drink and that might be the angle we needed.

When they finally made their way back to his home, we were still hanging out in the background taking extra precautions to avoid being spotted. Then he and the two bodyguards exited the car with the briefcase of collections and went inside. Then the two bodyguards left, and after that nothing...he stayed put...at home.

Pete let me off at the cabin. I decided to memorize the road and surrounding areas around the abandoned house and clearing. It was dark now, and I took the road apart until I knew every bump and pot hole. I knew exactly how long it would take to get there and back. After driving back and forth for the tenth time, I could read it like a book with my eyes closed. I got to the point where I could locate the house without seeing it or timing myself.

Pete and I continued to follow Tergandi for the entire week, but nothing came of it. He was always in the company of his bodyguards. And his itinerary varied a lot. He didn't seem to keep much of a recognizable routine, except for his collection days. It seemed almost impossible to lay our hands on him.

He drank, we knew that...and in excess, but it never seemed to be in the same place. If he decided to grab a meal, it always looked like a spur of the moment decision at whatever diner or restaurant was closest at the time. Nothing premeditated.

Once, he and his two bodyguards split up in two cars. Pete and I both looked at each other. His guess was as good as mine. We followed the car with the two of them in it. Guess what? When they got out, it was just the two bodyguards. He sure threw us off his trail. Where the fuck did he go? We didn't know, although I secretly wondered if it didn't have to do with some discreet female rendevous.

No wonder he's been on top for so long. He's shrewd, too shrewd. I was becoming a little impatient. Pete and I were practically waking him up in the morning and putting him to sleep at night but we couldn't get near him. Then, we realized how easy it was for him to lose us. Yeah, this was going to be rough.

CHAPTER 24

▼

MURDER

Chapter Twenty-Four

At the start of our second week our routine was much the same. Our man left his house with his bodyguards, we continued tagging him, but, still nothing. He was never alone for us to get near him. Then, after another wasted night, we were following him home when I noticed a faint shadow behind us. Peculiarly, it was another car with its lights out. The car suddenly speeded up and I barely had the chance to yell.

"Watch out, Pete!"

I reached for my gun and let go of the wheel, trying to hit the car's floor at the same time. I fell across Pete as I heard the thumping sound of bullets hitting the car's metal frame, and the smashing and breaking of glass pierced the air.

"The bastard's using a chopper," I shouted.

The car swerved from side to side with the screaming noise of tires biting into the concrete. The sound of metal against metal echoed in the night as the car hit something solid and came to a crashing halt.

I lay there on the floor with my gun in my hand for a few minutes, listening...the only sounds were night sounds and Pete's heavy breathing.

"Are ya hurt, Pete?"

"I must've caught a slug in the shoulder. I don't think it's too bad. How about you?"

"Just a few scratches, I think. Let's get the hell outta the car."

The door on my side was wedged in so badly that we had to squeeze out on Pete's side. I carefully got out and stood up, feeling dizzy as if all my bones were out of place. Pete's shoulder was bleeding but it was only a flesh wound. The car, however, was a total wreck.

We had crashed into a steel sign and had spun into the embankment. All the windows were shattered and the entire side of the car was riddled with bullet holes. It was a small wonder that the gas tank didn't blow.

We had three flats and I started to laugh. I had thought of a prank I had pulled on Joan's husband. One night, being cute and acting like a kid to impress Joan, I had let the air out of all his tires and gave him four flats. I kept laughing, thinking he still had one up on me. What a thing to think of at a time like this.

Pete gave me a peculiar look and I quickly had to reassure him.

"It's all right, Pete. I haven't flipped. I just thought of a private joke...well, my boy...what the fuck do we do now? We're gonna have a lot of explaining to do if a state trooper catches us here..."

"This is where the telephone company gets a chance to earn some money."

Pete walked to a pay phone booth not far away. When he returned, we waited about ten minutes and then a tow truck and car pulled up by us. Without a word, two men got out of the truck and went about their business quickly. They hooked up the car and backed it up a few feet. Then they both began cleaning up the debris. They even removed the sign and put it in the truck. When they finished all that remained of our accident were the skid marks. They even went over them and the skid marks disappeared.

"Beautiful job," I said. "Someone is gonna be awfully surprised and confused when they check this out and find nothing...you should get a doctor for your shoulder."

"I will, Tom."

Pete and I got into the other car, and were driven home. "It's lucky you saw him in time. I guess the bastard knows by now that we're on his tail."

"Well, he knows a car has been following him, but I doubt he knows who was in the car. We kept too good of a distance between us. You should take a few days off and give that shoulder a chance to mend. I'll continue watching him, but I'm gonna need another car."

"Take mine...it's outside your cabin. Here's the keys. But don't you think you'll need another man?"

"No, Pete. I don't think it'll be necessary. I'd rather handle it alone until you're okay."

"If you say so. But watch your ass..."

I continued tailing him, but it went nowhere, and this terribly, slow and unfruitful pace began wearing me down. I felt like my nerves were fraying. So, I decided to have a night off to get some release. I needed to get loaded, have a good round of drinks, relax, and then maybe I would be as good as ever to figure out what to do next.

So, I did. I broke my usual routine, left Tergandi behind, and headed straight for the bar near my cabin.

"You look tired, Tom. Something wrong?"

"No, Vi. Nothing that a good few shots won't cure."

Vi was the waitress there, and she readily brought the Jack Daniels to my table.

"What's going on in there?" There was music coming from the back room.

"They have a band playing there tonight. Nothing special. Do you want me to get you a table back there?"

"That's probably not necessary. I'll just get up and have a look."

"If you like it back there, Tom, let me know. I'll get you the best seat in the house."

I halted at the doorway at the back room and scanned the room. My glance fell on one particular table as my heart almost skipped a beat because sitting there were the Gold Dust twins, three women and my man, Frank Tergandi.

Well, I'll be damned. The one night I decided not to follow him, lady luck takes a hand and drops the bastard in my lap.

I sat down, near the doorway. Maybe tonight, was the night?

I called Vi over and asked if she would bring my drink over. It automatically reserved my seat. I then slipped out as if just going to the john. I sped to my car, re-parked it in a good spot behind the bar, and then removed my cool, steel of a forty-five from the glove compartment. I was ready now.

When I returned to the bar he was still sitting there and from the sound of their laughter, they were having a good time. I kept my eye on him constantly. Finally he stood up, said something to his companions and started towards my corner. He passed right by me and made a left turn into the men's room. Boy, was I lucky tonight!

I felt the excitement rise from my loins and flow through my body. This was it. This was the chance. It was the thrill of staying with your quarry, chasing and chasing him and then finally trapping him.

I followed him into the men's room after a few minutes, stepped inside and slipped my gun into his back as he was standing there taking a piss.

"Hi, Frank...don't do anything foolish...don't even fuckin' turn around...you just walk out the door, turn left instead of going through the bar and go out the back door...don't fuckin' try to even warn anyone."

No one paid us the slightest attention as we exited. We reached my car and I opened the door on the passenger's side.

"Get in," I said. "Slide over by the wheel."

He obeyed me in a manner so nonchalant that I was surprised and somewhat puzzled. This one didn't seem afraid. I slipped into the passenger's side next to him and handed him the keys to the car.

"Drive, Frank, and no tricks. Don't try to be a damn hero and you'll come out of this okay."

"Don't fuckin' worry. I'm not even gonna breath wrong...I don't like forty-fives pointing at me, especially with the safety off. Is this gonna be a one way ride?..."

He asked the question so casually. Did this one just hide his fear better or was he really unafraid? I wondered.

"You're very observant, aren't you? No, Frank, this is just a God damn warning. A little foretaste of what can and will happen, unless you leave my union alone...now, drive..."

"Which way?"

"Head towards the street and turn right. Keep going until I tell you to turn. Then make a left."

The car went rolling through as he followed my orders to a tee.

"Frank, I'm kind of curious. Did you order that hit the other night?"

"That was you? Of course, I did. I don't like fuckin' people following me. You were lucky. I might not miss next time."

"Next time?...You're an arrogant son of a bitch. I have the gun in my hand right now and I could kill you on the spot. It won't phase me one bit...turn left, next corner..."

I was taking him to the abandoned house that Pete had told me to check out. Although I couldn't see the house, I knew we just passed it.

"Stop the car here, Frank, nice and easy." I opened my door and backed out of the car keeping the gun aimed directly at him. "Move towards me and keep your hands high above your head where I can see 'em...walk towards those trees."

The moon was full and cast sufficient light for us to see into the clearing. After about twenty feet, I raised my hand and brought the gun crashing down behind his left ear. He uttered an involuntary cry of pain and fell unconscious. I kicked him a few times. He began to regain consciousness and tried to get up to swing at me.

I struck at him again and again and finally he collapsed. I watched his bloodied, crumpled body, motionless for the next few minutes. Not so fuckin' big now. I kicked him one more time.

I felt assured that he was really out unconscious and decided to leave him there. He'd be feeling those blows and broken ribs for some time. He was tough, but he didn't look that way now, and it was over. I could leave now.

I returned to my car and was just reaching for the car door's handle when the glass shattered before my eyes. I heard the echo of a shot. I whirled around and saw him lying on the ground aiming a gun.

I raised my gun and fired three shots, one after another. He was dead instantly.

You stupid motherfucker. Why the hell did you make me do it? Couldn't you just take the shit and leave well enough alone? Now you're nothing but a dead heap of shit. I only wanted to give you a fuckin' warning now look what you made me do."

I had to leave quickly. I jumped into the car and raced back to my cabin...a shovel...I had to find a shovel.

Everything came crashing in on me. I had to get back before the body was discovered. I had to hide the car because the window was blown out. I had to go back into the bar and pretend nothing happened.

I had finally done it. I finally committed murder. Well, it was the survival of the fittest. It always is. His shot could have killed me, and it could just as well been him burying me, right now. Imagine...Joan would never have known...might never have seen me again...he missed his target...me.

I was stupid. Should have searched him first...I should have...you stupid bastard...I should have...can't tell Pete...no one must know...if someone knows I just committed murder...if they talk...I'll fry...I have to get out...get out of the union completely...maybe, go back to Joan...convince her to leave town with me...

I finished digging the hole and rolled Frank's body into it. I was filled with horror. I heard a voice scream, then realized it was my own. I turned to look away, then I felt compelled to look at his body again...it was at this moment I knew I was through with the union...this time for good...

No, I probably would never be caught and convicted for this crime. But for the rest of my life I knew the image of his lifeless body and marred face would stick inside my head...I would tell Pete nothing...the first union rule that I learned was never talk about a murder, never get caught...we would just show up to tail him in the morning, and find out, no one was leaving...the guy was just missing...let Pete figure another enemy came along.

I filled the grave up with dirt, and crept out of the clearing so it looked as if no one had been there. When I drove away, I was positive no one would find him.

I got back to the hotel and proceeded to hide the car. Then I went straight into the bar and sat down.

Vi brought me a fresh drink. "Where did ya go, Tom?..."

"No place special. Just went back to my cabin...the band was so loud...grabbed a little shut eye."

"You missed the party."

"What?"

"Some big wheel was sitting in the back. Well, it seems he's missing. You should've seen how his companions practically turned this place inside out looking for him. You'd have thought he was the president himself...I say it was a woman...he looked the type."

"So he left with a woman. Probably wanted some privacy and a good time. You can't blame him..."

"Guess not..."

I went to a pay phone and tried to phone Joan. She wasn't home. Damn it, just when I needed her, I can't find her. I started drinking heavily. I had to rid my mind of that horrible picture of Frank's battered body and face...I returned to my cabin and packed my clothes...I called Pete and told him I couldn't stick around any longer. Made some excuse...told him where the car was and that I had hit a tree...I told him I was wanted back by John...very hush, hush...and, caught the next train, home...

C H A P T E R 25

▼

SECRETS

Chapter Twenty-Five

Secrets. Do I tell Joan? This was my dilemma. I was completely finished with the union but I made a horrible ending of everything. I knew that these last few weeks would never disappear and I would live to regret them for the rest of my life. I looked down at my hands and they were covered with blood. Ridiculous, there was nothing there, but I hid them underneath the table anyway.

"Hello, Joan," I said to my beloved Joan as I got up and kissed her.

"Tom, Tom…where have you been? Why did you go? Do you know how I've been tearing my hair out? It's been weeks…I didn't even know if you were dead."

"I don't see why I had to tell you. All we did was argue. You kept telling me to leave so often, I finally did."

"I didn't mean it, Tom. Forgive me, please. I missed you so much. No one knew where you were and I thought I had lost you. Then I realized how much I loved you."

"Marry me?"

I finally asked her.

There was a long pause as Joan burst into tears and smiles, clutching me tightly.

"Yes…" she cried out as I kissed her softly.

Well, I finally got to hold her forever. I had to come clean. The one thorn in my side was Frank's crumpled body and face. I couldn't shake it. And deep down inside, I felt it was only a matter of time before someone, somehow would find me.

"Honey. I heard of a place that I could buy. It's a bar and grill on Long Island. It isn't very expensive and I have the money. Y' know, I messed up. I thought I'd have one more fling with the union…that's all I had planned, but it turned out real bad. We could move…we should."

"This bad thing…did someone die?"

"Yeah, I'm afraid so. I was shot at. I didn't plan any of this. So I'm not a cold blooded murderer, okay? And there was no time to duck, or run. If I hadn't shot back I would be dead right now."

"Oh, Tom, this is terrible. Are they looking for you?"

"No one knows…but I wanna disappear…with you. Make a clean break. Honey, this is a terrible secret I have just shared with you. You must put it outta your mind completely, except I just don't wanna lie to you or keep secrets from you. Deep in my mind I know it was self-defense...I keep telling myself it wasn't my fault...you must believe me...and forgive me. I should never have put our relationship in jeopardy."

"It's okay, Tom," she said softly. "This isn't going to change anything. This will just make our love stronger. This terrible thing has happened to us now, and I mean, us. What happens to you, happens to me. Do you understand how much I love you? Just don't go away again...never again."

I held her hand tightly and looked into her eyes.

"Joan, you don't know what this means to me...when can we get married?"

"In Long Island," she said laughing lightly. "And I have to make you an honest man. We really do have to wait for my divorce to be final."

"I wanna spend the rest of my life with you, Joan. Maybe we should go to Reno. It takes too long to get a divorce in this state...then we can get married, anywhere. I'm gonna put down a payment for the bar and grill today...we can change our names and make it even harder for anyone to find us."

She looked at me concerned and worried. "But honey, that would be running away. You've never been afraid of anything in your life..."

"Yes Joan, I am running and I am afraid but I'm severing all ties with the union...for us...and from all the people I have known there. But the union might find us here. They might decide they need me. It's a funny business. Y' know how they operate. If they have something on you, they can and will hold it over your head. If we stay in this town, we'll be pushing our luck.

"I'm a marked man, Joan. You don't know how many nasty assignments I've had and in how many different places. It's only a matter of time before they find me. If it wasn't for you I wouldn't care in the least. But you're the one...God has finally given me a new chance...not many people get that. You're my happiness, and besides, if you want to call it running, it's running for a future.

"I have it all figured out. You go to Reno and I'll go buy the bar and grill. I'm gonna change my name to Romano. I'll take another driver's test in another state for a license under that name. I have a friend...he can get me another social security card and that's all we'll need...when you get back, free and clear, we can get married, go pick out a house out there, and you'll be, the beautiful Mrs. Joan Romano...and, don't be scared. This really is the best thing. It's for a new life for us."

"I know, Tom. It's okay."

"Think of it hon, a different identification, new names and a brand new life. Anything we can do…I have to get away from the union and the past."

"Okay, Tom…let's do it…I can leave tomorrow. No, I can leave today. I'll get the divorce in Reno. Let's just be together, and you never go back to them."

And she did. She was my jewel. She was worth all the pain and worry. I sometimes do not know why God can be so kind.

CHAPTER 26

▼

THE PAST RETURNS

Chapter Twenty-Six

I knew there was no other man in the world who was as happy as me when I woke up on our first anniversary. Joan was lying next to me with a smile on her face. Her beauty was radiant and I knew she was happy as well.

This past year had been good to us. We had our new home and Romano's was booming. The money was rolling in and it was clean money. My past was behind us and buried, the people in the town accepted us, and, although we worried in the beginning, happiness and contentment surrounded us. Yes, I felt we were blessed.

I leaned over and gently kissed her on her lips. Joan stirred and slowly opened her eyes.

"Good morning, hon," she said sleepily.

"Happy anniversary, darling. Did I tell you I love you today?…"

"Well, if you did, I would only pretend I didn't hear, just to get you to say it again."

"I do love you, and, I have a present for you on our first anniversary…how would you like a vacation…a real vacation? How about Chicago, Cuba, the Bahamas, California?…."

She sat up quickly, but the surprise written all over her face, soon faded.

"What about our business? How can we just take off?"

"Oh, don't worry your pretty little face about that. Jake can take care of the business while we're away. I'll just pay him an extra bonus…now, just as fast as you can, start packing. We can leave and have the time of our lives…"

It was our second honeymoon, and it was to last two months. We went everywhere…sight-seeing, beach combing, casino cruising, dining, dancing, listening to jazz, taking in all the shows…we took long walks in the moonlight, and danced with the stars above us as company. Sometimes we just stayed in bed all day.

Joan had made my life so happy. I just wanted her to have the very best and anything she wanted. I could never put a price tag on our past year of happiness, and these two months were bliss…

We walked back into Romano's, suntanned, rested, happy…chatting away like school kids as Jake waved at us.

"Boss, Mrs. Romano, you look great! How was your trip?"

"We had a wonderful time. Thank you, Jake. I'll show you all the photos later…Tom, I'm going to check in on the kitchen and talk a little back there…with the waitresses…you know…"

"Business looks good, Jake." I glanced throughout the room and even though the lights were dim, I could see that the place was filled to capacity.

"Yeah, Tom. It's been booming. It's been like this practically every night. You need to check the books?"

"Later, Jake. Think I'll have a drink first."

I sat down at the bar. Jake had the seat reserved, the one I liked best because it gave me a view of the whole place, dance floor, booths, tables and all.

"Hi, boss. Nice to see ya back…the usual?"

"Thanks, Bernie. The usual will be fine."

"Nice crowd, boss. We've been doing well. Very busy."

The floor show ended and the lights brightened slightly. My eyes scanned the room as I daydreamed about Joan again, then I silently gasped. At a table to the right, sat Sallie and Sheila, and my whole world started to fall into little pieces.

The moment I saw him I was frightened. I imagined everything I had built up being torn down in an instant and smashed like a pane of glass. I slowly turned around so that my back faced his table. Another drink helped calm me. I intended to ignore him and thought of slipping out the back, grabbing Joan and leaving. I should've.

But I remembered. I remembered what good friends we had been once…all the times he bailed me out of shit. The big favor he did for me once…the time he risked his own life for me…I should go over there and at least say hello. Besides, I had to find out what he was doing here. Was it coincidence? Did John send him here? Did he know where I was? I had to find out if he was here on business. Did he mean me any harm?

"Hello, Sallie. It's been a long time."

Sallie looked up at me and practically jumped out of his seat. I thought he was going to piss his pants and his surprise…recognizing me…made him almost appear ridiculous. Then a grin broke out and his face lit up.

"Tom, you son of a bitch…what the hell are you doing here? Where in the world did you come from?…Here sit down, join us. You remember my wife, Sheila?"

"Of course, I do. How are you Sheila? Still the best cook this side of the Hudson? I never will forget the wonderful meal you cooked for me…it was so long ago."

"Too long. Thanks, Tom. I do remember you. Only you look so different now…happy…hey Sal…," she turned to her husband. "Bet it's a girl. Did you finally find someone and settle down?"

I had exactly two seconds to decide how to play this conversation. The longer we talked, the more likely they would catch on about my name change and everything. If I said nothing, would Sallie play along? Perhaps Sheila wouldn't remember my old last name.

"Yeah, I did…finally meet someone, someone wonderful. It's only been a year but it's the best thing that happened to me…here, order what you like…it's on the house."

"On the house?" Sheila gasped.

"Life has been good to me. I own this place."

"Holy shit Tom, that's just great. What a break for you."

"Thanks. What brings you both out here, by the way?"

"I have an office in the city now. No more selling on the road for me. Sheila and I were thinking about buying a house here. This seems like a nice town."

Sallie pierced my gaze. His eyes were pleading with me. What was he trying to tell me? All at once, I remembered…Sheila never knew about the union. His eyes were begging me to remember this and I had gotten the message in time. I guess, I relaxed as well. If I could keep his secret, he could keep mine.

"Yeah, Sallie. I agree. This is a nice town. I have a big stake here. I'm married, I have my own home, and the people here like this place, and I'm gonna make sure it stays that way."

"Excuse me," Sheila said as she got up from her chair. "You two must have a lot to talk about so I'll just go powder my nose."

We waited until she left, then began whispering to each other.

"Sallie, before you say anything. I changed my name. Furcco doesn't exist anymore…and no one is supposed to know where I am…do you understand?…It's a little like your secret with Sheila. She doesn't know about you either, right?"

"Tom, Tom. Don't worry. I'm just so glad to see you. Everyone wondered what had happened to you. We all thought you got whacked…well, as far as I'm concerned Thomas Furcco is dead. If you want it dead, let's keep it that way…and, no, I didn't know you were here. We decided to stop by here by accident…and I have no intention of telling anyone…imagine, here you are, a respected businessman. I'm glad for you, Tom…I'm glad you got out…I wish I could fuckin' get out…"

"Thanks Sallie. You keep this to yourself. Y' know, my wife knows all about my past, but we decided to change our name and move, and put it all behind us. This is our new life. I'm respected here. I've made something outta my life and it's a clean, decent life. If you want to see me again, that's up to you. But, remember, no union, no talking about it all. I don't even want to know how John is. I've erased it all. But you and me, we were always close friends. I trust you…however, you must be very careful when you come here, I don't want anybody on your tail, especially old Dave. So be very careful Sallie…by the way is he still around? Not close by, I hope."

"Dave? Dave is still around…he looked for you for a long time. I'm sure he thinks you were whacked by now, like everyone else, but he's in the city sometimes…he and I still come to blows…"

"Just be careful…as I said."

"Tom, let the dead stay dead…I wish I had the balls to get out…y' know, how it is…I don't think Dave travels much outta the city, though…"

"I don't go to the city…"

"Well, he's managed to get himself in with some other union. Big mistake in my opinion, but they need a goon that they've got something on. I'll pass the word around…see if I can keep him so busy, he won't ever show up in this direction…forget about him, Tom. I don't want to open old wounds."

"Sallie, we've been friends for such a long time. I cannot forget and toss aside the countless times you were there for me. We've been through so much together…"

"Tom, as I said before, I don't want to interfere in your new life."

"So, we can still be friends. Just don't talk shop. And don't talk to anyone. I'm not going back, ever…"

"Don't fuckin' worry. Sheila still doesn't know either. As far as she's concerned, I'm an advertising executive. And that's that."

"So it's settled. We still keep our friendship."

"Yeah…"

Sheila returned and sat down.

"You boys have a good talk?"

"We sure did…"

"Look, you two. After you get settled and buy your house, how about coming to my place for dinner sometime? I want you to meet my wife, Joan."

"We'd love to, Tom."

"In fact, how about next Wednesday? I just have to check with Joan first. How about you give me a call here, oh, let's say, sometime after five PM, tomorrow or the next day?"

"Alright, Tom. We'll pencil it in and give you a call."

"Good...I know Joan will be glad to meet both of you. This will be great. And, Sallie, don't be a stranger around here."

"We'll be in touch, Tom."

CHAPTER 27

▼

DISAPPEARANCE

Chapter Twenty-Seven

Joan and I returned home and I remained pensive. I couldn't sleep either. I tried to read a book, but my thoughts kept wandering back over meeting up with Sallie after all this time. Joan stirred a little and then woke up.

"Having trouble sleeping, hon?"

"Joan, I ran into a very, old friend at the bar. His wife too. He's buying a house here and I invited them to dinner next Wednesday. Is that okay with you? I hope you don't mind."

"Of course, I don't mind, Tom. You don't need my permission to bring people here to our home. If I'm too tired to cook, I'll just have the restaurant bring something over."

"I think I need your permission on this friend...honey...I know we buried my past a long time ago...I didn't plan this...it's Sallie, the man I worked with in the union."

Joan kind of sank down as her face shivered slightly.

"Oh, no, Tom, It's not coming back to hurt us, is it? We've been so happy. I don't want things to change. This isn't a good idea. He's going to bring back the entire past again."

"No, honey. He won't. I talked to him about this. He knows that Tom Furcco is dead forever. Y' know, his own wife doesn't even know he works for the union. And he doesn't want her to know. We can keep his secret and he'll keep ours. We discussed this. The union, my past, or even mention of the union is taboo for him."

"I don't know, Tom. I'm afraid."

"I have his word on this and I know he's a man of his word. He's always been a loyal friend and he's gotten me out of more bad scrapes than I care to remember...no, honey. We have nothing to fear. I'm sure of that...when you meet him, don't associate him with the union. Think of him as a new friend, a person you've never heard of before. It'll make things easier..."

"Alright, Tom. I'll try. But, I'm still afraid for us...just try to understand that."

I took her in my arms and kissed her.

"Honey, I'm very happy...you are my world, y' know...I would never let anything or anyone interfere with our happiness and new life here."

Joan took to Sheila immediately when they came over for dinner. But she was a little hesitant with Sallie. However, my worst fears disappeared quickly. As the evening wore on, her coolness subsided. She began to find him likable, and we all soon had the beginnings of a warm and friendly relationship. The friendship that had existed between Sallie and me over the years had now spread amongst the four of us.

We began to see more of each other. Joan had a new girlfriend, and so did Sheila. Sallie visited the club frequently, and true to his word, the union was never mentioned. That is until one day when he walked into my place and started drinking heavily.

"You kind of look worn out, tired, Sallie. What the hell's wrong?"

"It's that bastard, Dave…he's givin' me a rough time. Look, Tom, I don't wanna bring this up…I just wish I had someone to talk to…"

I held up my hand to halt the conversation, and pointed to my mouth making a zip it up gesture.

"Sallie, I can't. I promised Joan, and you gave me your word. I can't help you."

"I know that, Tom. And, believe me, I wouldn't want you to. It's just that everywhere I turn lately, I run into a brick wall."

"Listen, Sallie. Just because you're my friend, I'll listen. But make it quick and that's all I can do…just hear you out, but I have no advice."

"He's moving in on me and moving fast. It's always the shops. He fuckin' wants 'em all and we can't seem to settle this personal beef. He's become vicious. He sends death threats, fixes people's cars, has people beaten up. The situation is dangerous now. I'm at the end of my rope, and there doesn't seem to be any solution except to…well, you would know what the solution is…again, I have to kill someone?…"

"Sallie, why the hell don't you just get the hell out of the union? You can walk away just like I did. If you need some extra money, or some other kind of help, I'll give it to you. You can count on me…maybe you should sell the house and move to another state…how about the Carolinas or Virginia?…California?…"

"I can't get out. I told you, I haven't the fuckin' balls…it's too complicated. I can't run and hide…how would I explain this to Sheila? She would surely leave me. They've had me for too long. They'd find me. I'd have to keep packing up and keep running. I don't think I could take it. And Sheila? Do you see her moving every six months, just leaving everything behind every time? Maybe it would be different if she knew, had always known…no, I can't do it."

"Well, Sallie, don't you think I had those fears too? I was sorry I joined the damn union. Don't you know that I know, the only retirement from the union is a fuckin' casket. Yeah I'm in hiding, but I'm doing okay. I wish you would rethink this. I want you out...but honestly, if you've tried everything with the bastard, you already know there's only one alternative. And, I can't help you there."

"I know. I just needed to tell someone. I'll be okay. I'm always careful...thanks...at least for listening to me."

It was after that conversation that Sallie made himself scarce. I thought of getting in touch with him, but I hesitated. I should've. I'm always saying that. I should've. I should've never walked over to talk to them. Never should've listened to his union problem. I should've kept at him, trying to convince him to get out.

Weeks later, the phone rang while I was at home.

"Hello, Tom? This is Sheila....Sal hasn't come home yet. He's been missing for two days now. I'm worried and I don't know what could've happened to him, and I looked up his office number...in the phone book..." She started to cry.

"Don't get so upset, Sheila. He probably just has a lot of work to do and has stayed at a hotel."

"But, I called the number in the book. They have no Salvatore Toccola working for them...what am I gonna do?"

"Maybe you just called the wrong number. Didn't he give you a number?"

"I lost the number he gave me...it's not like Sal to lie to me...something is wrong, I just know it...I even checked with the hospitals, in case it was a car accident...but nothing."

"Take it easy, Sheila. Why don't you come over here and stay with Joan? I tell ya what. I'll take a ride into the city and see if I can find him. Y' know, he probably just tied one on with the boys and is sleeping it off somewhere. Don't worry."

"Ok, Tom. Thanks. I'll be right over. I'm sorry to bother you, but I have nowhere else to turn."

An old, familiar feeling came over me, and built up so fast that I was almost panicking. I didn't like it. Something was wrong. Sallie could be in trouble. It was union business, wasn't it? Could be nasty.

"What's the matter, hon?"

Joan walked into the room. She hadn't heard our phone conversation, but she could tell from the expression on my face, that something was wrong.

"That was Sheila. Sallie hasn't been home for two days and she's worried about him. She's afraid something may have happened to him, so I told her to come over here and stay with you, and that I'd try to find him."

"No, Tom. Don't go. Tell her to call the damn police."

"Y' know she can't, Joan. Suppose it's some nasty union business? Do you want him to spend the rest of his life in jail?"

"Please, don't go, Tom. I don't want anything to happen to you...I knew it. I knew it. When you first told me you ran into your old friend, didn't I tell you he was going to stir something up?...Ruin our new life here..."

I took her in my arms and held her tight.

"Nothin' is going to happen to me...Sallie's probably out drunk somewhere. He gets that way every once in a while. Anyway, he's my friend. She has no one else to turn to, Joan. I'll just pay a little visit to his office...see if anyone seen him."

After thinking about it for a few minuets, she said softly. "Ok, Tom." There were tears in her eyes.

"I'm making too much of this, I guess. You know best. Just please be careful. And, call me when you get in the city."

"Don't worry. I'm sure there's no need to be alarmed. I'll just drive to the city and if I don't return here with Sallie, it'll be because he already came home. Now cheer up."

As I drove to the city, I realized I didn't have the least idea where to look for Sallie. Did something happen to him? Did Dave grab him? He had worked himself up pretty high in the union, so I doubt he was on an assignment. He would send someone else. He gave out assignments now. No, more than likely he's steamed up about something and went on drinking spree. Of course, he could be in hiding for some reason...but he would've called Sheila and given her some explanation...or, he'd have someone else call her to keep her from talking and worrying...he's not fuckin' stupid....

That's why I was getting worried. He didn't call. Reluctantly, I knew exactly where I had to start. But I couldn't. I couldn't just show up at the union office, not after all these years. I'd ruin my cover...I'd ruin my life with Joan...I couldn't...think, Tom, think.

I decided to go to Sallie's office instead and bluff a little. I rummaged through the glove compartment. There it was...next to the letter to Joan, although that was something else. He had given me his office address a while back and I had written it down and hid it in the car. Just in case.

I didn't know the people at his office. I was more familiar with John Gervonte's crew. I decided to risk being spotted. After all, he was my friend. And I know he'd do the same for me.

Upon entering the office I could see Sallie wasn't exaggerating when he told me he had a big staff. I walked over to the receptionist's desk, and told her why I was there. I told her that Sallie's wife was hysterical, and had asked me to go to her husband's office and ask around...he was missing for two days now.

I was right. A little bit of the truth went a long way and the secretary became visibly upset. Before I could speak further, she jumped out of her chair and said, "Follow me."

We went down a long corridor, and all she did was put her fingers to her tightly closed lips, meaning, no one should talk. We stopped outside a door and she knocked gently on it. She pointed that I should wait, and walked in herself, closing the door very quietly.

A few minutes later, she and a husky looking man appeared. They still indicated no talking, and he pointed to the end of the corridor, pulling my arm in that direction. The both of us went down a flight of stairs, and out into an alley. He kept walking and I followed. Finally, after walking down a few streets, he stopped at a bar, and we both went in.

He chose a back table where the lights were dim, but the juke box was loud. After sitting down, he snapped his fingers at a waiter, and then spoke for the first time.

"We have to be very careful...Feds...They took an office in my building...but I'm not supposed to know about it. Fuckin' Fed's! No privacy. So, you know Sallie?..."

"I can't stay for long, so I'll have to make this quick. Do y' know where he could be? His wife hasn't heard from him in two days. I can't tell you who I am and you will have to forget my face and this conversation when I leave..."

"I have to know who you are, but, I haven't seen him either. He told me nothing."

"When did you see him last? Was it at your office? Can you remember exactly?"

"Hmm…yes, the office…well, no. It was at Myer's Bar, two days ago, around six-seven P.M. We had a few drinks. He left first."

"Did you see anyone approach him? Did he hail a cab?"

"No, nothing unusual. I assumed he was going home. I guess, in his own car."

"Do you know anything about him having trouble with Dave?"

He looked shocked when I asked him this.

"How the fuck do you know that? Who the hell exactly are you?"

The mysterious, husky man from Sallie's office got up from his chair abruptly.

"Listen," I lowered my voice and urged him to sit down again.

"I used to work with Sallie. I'm on the run. If the police ever catch me, it's the fuckin' slammer for sure…OKAY?…Now, I'm one of his emergency phone calls. He saved my damn life once. If he needs the favor returned, I'd get a call. Well, I did—only it was from his wife."

The guy breathed a big sigh.

"Okay. Call me Marty for now. I guess I'll take a chance on this being true. We know he's missing. I don't know where. We checked the hospitals and morgue, the recent arrests at the stations, but again, nothing. I have people looking for him right now, but so far we've hit a dead end…he just fuckin' disappeared."

"Could Dave have him?"

"Dave and Sallie had this personal beef for months. For some time now things have been bad."

"Could Dave have killed him, or had him killed?"

"Doubt it. Grabbed maybe, but he wouldn't kill him."

"How do you know?"

Marty looked at me again, breathed a big sigh. I got the feeling I wasn't trusted, but I had to see what I could pry out of him without showing all my cards.

"Marty, it's very important." I took a hundred dollar bill out of my wallet and stuck it in his hand.

"You must be a pretty good friend? Alright, I'll tell you about Dave. He won't kill Sallie because of the contracts. I don't know if any of this is gonna make sense to you, but here's the little information I can give you. Sallie has to sign these contracts, only Sallie's signature, could give Dave control. Sallie had the lawyers draw up the contracts that way. Only his signature. It's all legal and no one can break the contract without his approval. The only way Dave can get anything is if Sallie signs it over to him. That's the only thing I can come up with."

"What happens if Sallie dies?"

"The contracts are taken over by the New York office. Whoever replaces Sallie will have the same power…so there's nothing to gain by killing him."

"Does Dave know this arrangement?"

"Yeah. Dave knows. Everyone knows Sallie's setup."

"Then, it looks like Dave might have Sallie, unless he's just drunk somewhere."

"I don't think he's drinking with Dave on his fuckin' ass. Anyway, we checked the local bars down here. But even when Sallie's on a spree, or a job, he always had sense enough to keep in touch with his wife. He was dead set against her knowing about his job. So he'd always let her know just how long he'd be away from home…yeah, it's fuckin' Dave, isn't it?"

"Can you get me any information on where Dave hangs out? Where would he take someone if he grabbed him and wanted to rough him up a little?"

"I don't know. I can ask around…see what I get…by the way, what's your name? How do I get in touch with you?"

"You can just call me George. And, I'll get in touch with you. Can you trust your secretary?" He nodded.

"If you're not at your office when I stop by next, leave the information with her, okay? See if you can get some information by tonight. And thanks, Marty. Thanks a lot."

When I walked back into my living room, I found Joan and Sheila sitting there looking like they had seen a ghost. Sheila had apparently been crying. I walked over to Joan and kissed her.

"Why don't you fix me a drink?" I said softly, collapsing into a chair. I put my hands across my eyes and I realized how tired I was. And I had no good news to give anyone. Everyone was silent. This went on for several long minutes.

"Sheila, I didn't find Sallie yet. But I will. I talked with someone from his office. They are making calls around town to see where he went…I'm sure it was just a drinking spree. He's probably sleeping it off somewhere…"

"I don't know, Tom. He always calls. A whole two days, and nothing. No, something is wrong. I'm going home. I've been back and forth, between here and my house, just in case he called."

"Sheila? Can I ask you a question?"

"Huh?"

"What do you really know about your husband? I mean his work."

"Well, he's in advertising. He's an executive. He always was a great sales-man. I guess he handles advertising accounts now."

"Are you sure?"

"What's with all these questions? Where is my damn husband?"

Sheila crumpled somehow into a frail, small figure and started to sob again.

"I should call the police. Maybe he's been robbed...maybe someone beat him up for his wallet or car or something..."

"Sheila, you may not want to call the police."

"Why's that? Of course, I should. I just thought I'd see him walking through the door by now."

"Well, Sheila. I'm sorry you have to find out the truth at a time like this, but it's time, I guess, for you to know that the type of work Sallie does is not advertising."

"What are you talking about? You don't make any sense. What is this a joke to you? Where's my husband? This is a nightmare..."

"Sheila, you're getting hysterical. Now stop this...hear me out. I think Sallie could be in big trouble. I'm gonna find him and get him outta this mess. But when I bring him back to you, I want you to promise me that you both will move, go start a new life somewhere."

"I don't understand anything you're saying."

"I just want you to promise. Promise you'll stay with him and do what-ever it takes to get him going in a new direction. Sheila! Your husband works for a union. They call him a gangster..."

Her face froze and stayed that way, with tears slipping down one after another. She looked a mess, a twisted tangle of emotions, surprise, fright, grief, and disbelief. It was sometime before she could bring herself to speak.

"No..." It was a drawn out syllable that got stuck in the back of her throat. I sat down besides her and took her hand.

"Listen, Sheila. He told me. He never wanted you to know. That's how much he loves you. He never wanted you to worry—all those supposed busi-ness trips...he wanted you to just have a beautiful life with all the pretty things you wanted. He just didn't want you to know...he has a dirty job and he just wanted you to only see something beautiful...can you understand that?"

"Why, why didn't he ever tell me?

She sobbed and quietly talked out loud.

"Why Sal? I'd rather have been poor and happy with you. Why? And now what?…He could be lying in the gutter somewhere."

"Sheila, I know this is a big shock for you. But can you understand that you have to get him outta this business?"

"Yes," she shook her head and still sobbed.

"You have to be brave. And, promise me. You'll both leave town. Move out of state, even change your names. And stick by him. He needs you. I'm going to find him. I promise you."

"And, if something happens to you? No, I could never look Joan in the face. Don't go. I shouldn't have involved you. These gangsters, they're dangerous, aren't they? No, don't go. Let me go home. I have to think."

"That's okay, Sheila. You need some rest. Joan, why don't you stay with her tonight? She can use your sweet, caring touch."

"Of course, I will…it will be alright Sheila. First, you need a good night's sleep." Joan stood on her tip toes and kissed me.

"Don't go," Joan whispered.

"You take care of Sheila. I'm still gonna find him. Sallie's my friend, y' know. Someone has to know something. But I'll be careful. Don't worry."

Sheila started out the door staring listlessly into the setting sun. Joan hung back for a second.

"Don't, Tom, please."

"Honey, I only intend to try to find some information on his whereabouts. Then I'll either turn it over to the union or to the police. I'll be fine."

"I'm afraid, Tom. I have a feeling that something awful is gonna happen." Her arms were around me. She was holding me so tightly, a gale of wind couldn't have whipped her away from me.

"Stop worrying. You're gonna make yourself sick with this needless worry. Now, stop it. Sheila needs your compassion and strength right now. I'll be fine. I love you."

"I love you too."

Joan wiped a tear from her face and joined Sheila outside. I watched them for a while, two fragile figures, arms around each other, getting smaller and smaller as they walked away into the fading light.

For some reason, I felt strangely better, not worried at all like Joan. The two women had each other and would be okay while I was gone. I began to wonder if God wasn't giving me another chance this way. It was I who was being sent to find Sallie, wasn't it? Maybe it was a way to atone for some of the terrible atrocious acts I had committed, crimes the law never stretch out its arms to seize or punish me about. And I was lucky about that.

And now, for the third time in my life, I had found someone, Joan, so sweet and good...Mary and Connie? I had gotten over them finally. How else could I say thank you, God for giving me my Joan. And, Sallie was my friend. This would eat into my conscience, if I didn't go look for him. I wouldn't be able to live with myself...I wouldn't be able to live with anyone...can I imagine living at all, without my Joan?

Our happiness will no longer be threatened. No, I had to find Sallie and get him back. I wanted to give him the chance I had...I would find him and get him out of the union. I wanted to say thank you to God somehow this way.

I went into my study where my gun was hidden, then left.

CHAPTER 28

▼

HUNTING SALLIE

Chapter Twenty-Eight

I drove back into the city. First stop, Sallie's office. I wanted to get there before everyone left. Marty was not there. The secretary was just packing up. She looked up at me and fished out her keys. From her desk drawer she removed a small envelope and handed it to me.

"Late night for me...I have to get going and lock up."

I left quickly...in and out. Never give them much time to know where you are. I was lucky to have gotten there before they had all left. Inside the envelope Marty had written down Dave's home address. I guess that was all the information he had found so far.

So, this is what I'll do. If Dave had something to do with Sallie's disappearance, I would stake out Dave's home. Dave must've moved in on Sallie before Sallie had a chance to play his hand. I mapped out my plan. All I had to do was tail Dave and maybe, just maybe, he would lead me to Sallie...

I picked up a good strong cup of coffee, then found Dave's address. I parked almost a block away from his home making sure the house entrance was within sight. I had no idea how long I would sit there, but again, I got lucky. Within about fifteen minutes, I spotted him leaving.

He hadn't changed much. As I watched from a distance, I felt that old, buried hate rise up inside of me again. He was accompanied by two men and they headed to his car and drove away. I followed, at least five cars' lengths behind them, but never let their car out of my sight.

They stopped at a diner and grabbed a quick meal. I waited. I had to hang back because I was sure that he would recognize me. I couldn't afford that, him and me tangling with each other instead of my locating Sallie.

When they left the diner, they hopped back in the car and headed into the tunnel for New Jersey. Fortunately, there was enough traffic between us to keep them from sighting me. I stayed with them for about twenty miles, when finally, their car turned off into a driveway and drove past a sign reading "Motel and Cabins for Rent."

I drove slowly past the place and kept going. I looked the landscape over. It was deserted except for a motel and a gas station down the road. I turned around and headed back to the motel, checking to see where they had parked.

I asked for a cabin and checked in. I had cabin, number ten, all the way down the road. I took my gun out of the glove compartment and made sure it was loaded properly. Then I started for where I had seen their car.

A small, sliver of light showed at the end of the road. As I neared it, I seen a cabin which was separated from the others, somewhat tucked in and hard to spot. Their car was parked nearby and I looked to see if anyone was around. I saw no one so I moved along side their car. It was empty, but there on the front seat was the outline of something familiar. How convenient I thought. I reached in and my hand fell on cold metal. It was a forty-five and it felt loaded.

I slipped it in my pocket and crouched down behind the car trying to get a closer view of the cabin. I listened for sounds but heard nothing.

My first instinct, was to go get help. Sallie could be anywhere here. Even dead. But, I decided I needed to see or hear him, and be positive first. I crept along the ground to the front window so rapidly and noiselessly that I couldn't even hear myself move. I glanced through a tiny opening in the blinds as my own pulse quickened.

There was Sallie tied to a chair with Dave standing over him. Dave raised his arm and crashed his fist into Sallie's face. His head jerked sideways and a trickle of blood flowed freely out of his mouth. Sallie looked like he had just said something. Whatever it was, Dave laced right into him again. I counted four other men in the room. I had to go get help.

Just as I took a step towards the trees, the door suddenly opened and a shaft of light brightened the whole area in front of the cabin. I was caught unawares and barely made it around the side of the cabin.

Dave and the two men left and got into their car. I heard Dave's voice, "He'll come round. Tomorrow we'll fuckin' work him over again. He'll be begging us to let him sign."

His voice faded into the night as the car drove off.

I remained standing against the building, and waited for my breath to slowly return to normal. I crept around to the front of the cabin and looked through the window again. Sallie was in a semi-conscious state and looked in bad shape. One of the remaining men was sitting on the bed and the other was playing a lone game of cards.

Now was my chance to get him out. I only had two goons to get rid of and Dave said he wouldn't be back until tomorrow. These guys wouldn't be expecting anyone, so I'd have surprise on my side.

A plan, Tom. Think of a plan. I could crash the door. That would be easy. I would have exactly two or three seconds. I would have to shoot and be very accurate, get them both before they had time to react.

I advanced to the door with my gun in my hand, I took hold of the door-knob, butted my shoulder against the door, twisted the doorknob and shoved the door open. The man playing cards froze, one hand still holding a card in mid air. I got him first.

The other stood up quicky as his hand darted to his jacket pocket. My trigger finger moved mechanically in his direction and the room shook with a deafening roar as I continued firing. He started to go down, staring vacantly at me, then began reeling. He made a desperate attempt to grasp the wall as his gun dropped from his limp hand. Blood oozed from his chest and he half stood there momentarily before finally tumbling.

I turned quickly to check the other guy. He stared back at me with fear written all over his face.

"Don't move," I said as I backed up to shut the door. I kept my gun pointed at him while I moved warily in his direction. Then I hit him behind the ear waiting for his head to hit the table. I quickly went to Sallie, and began cutting him loose.

"You alright, Sallie?"

"They been fuckin' around with me a lot but I'm still in one piece. You know, I thought you would search for me, but I hoped you wouldn't."

"The hell with it, Sallie. Let's get the fuck outta here. We haven't time for a formal chat."

We heard the sound of a car suddenly. I opened the door a crack and saw headlights piercing the night. The car came to a sudden halt near the trees and three men got out. I shut the door quickly.

"It's fuckin' Dave...he came back."

What an asshole Tom. I felt for the bulge of the spare gun.

"Stupid, fuckin' idiot...I really did it this time. They must've realized the gun in their car was missing...I took it."

"Don't worry, Tom. We'll make it."

I quickly scanned the room hoping to find another exit. There was none, except through a window but, there wasn't enough time for that. Sallie pulled the light switch and the room was enveloped in darkness. Dave must of realized something was wrong when he seen the cabin go dark.

Through the window, little spears of flames erupted from the darkness beyond the trees as I heard them...wham, wham, wham, the bullets banged against the cabin.

I threw Sallie the spare gun. The room shattered with explosions as Sallie began returning their fire.

"Get down, you damn fool," I yelled at him. He crawled on his hands and knees to reach me.

"Tom, the only way out is through the door."

"I know Sallie. And it's gonna be rough making a break for it...I saw one of the men by the tree on the right side of us."

"There's one by the car, too."

"That's two of 'em. Where the hell is the third one? I saw three get outta the car."

"I don't know, Tom. He must be behind the trees."

We held our fire, and when they stopped shooting, a deathly quiet arrived. Then Dave's voice boomed from a distance.

"Who the fuck's in there. Come out. I don't wanna hurt you....I'm give you a minute to think it over..."

Sallie and I continued to talk in whispers.

"Look, Tom. We both have wives. Our lives are important, more important than a hundred shops. The hell with the union. I'm gonna sign the damn papers. Let's tell 'em we get clear passage outta here first."

"Sallie, you're forgetting one thing. Dave doesn't know who's in here with you, but when he finds out it's me, he's gonna wanna bury me. He won't let me go...

"You know how I hurt him once. He lost a shop and spent a long time in the hospital because of me. He'll have nothing but revenge on his mind. He never crossed me off his hate lists...no, Sallie. I'll tell you what we'll do. You get the hell outta here while I cover you. Then, I'll hold them off until you come back with help."

"The hell with you, Tom. We're in this together and we'll leave together. You risked your life coming here, and I'm not leaving you behind. What the fuck do you take me for? After all these years, you think that I'll turn my back on you?"

"Alright, Sallie. Tell him you'll sign if we get clear passage outta here."

"Dave," Sallie shouted. "I'm willing to sign, but we want safe passage outta here. You clear your men out first. I'll meet you in your office in an hour...I give you my word on this."

"Yeah, yeah. Who the fuck you got in there with you Sal?"

"Does it make a difference?"

"Let me hear his voice."

"I'm no one you know."

"Dave, the important thing is the shops will be yours. Do we have a deal?"

"That other voice…sounds familiar…Tom? Is that you? You bastard!" he screamed with hate. "I fuckin' have you where I want you…no, no, no deal…you weren't included in my plans."

"Dave, you can have the shops. This will make you a big earner with the New York Boss's, and it will put you in good with your own boss," Sallie continued trying to negotiate.

"Fuhgeddaboutit," he shouted back. "This is what I'll do. You can go, Sallie. But not you, Tom. Tom and I have an unfinished personal beef….that's my last offer."

"Fuck you!" Sallie yelled back.

CHAPTER 29

▼

GUN FIRE

Chapter Twenty-Nine

"This is your chance, Sallie. I can hold 'em off until you get back with help...go, Sallie." I watched his face in the thin flicker of moonlight that filtered through the window. Not even a muscle moved.

"No, Tom...you're in this mess because of me and I'm not running out on you...Tom, be serious...they'll slaughter you...I know this guy...I doubt he'll even let you go...no, we'll fight this out together."

"Well, are you coming out?" Dave's voice boomed.

"Come and get us, you cock-sucker."

"Alright, you bastard...we will."

A barrage of bullets started splattering against the doorway and I had to dive to the floor. The firing stopped as suddenly as it had begun, and once again, it was quiet. The door was partially open and you couldn't see anything in the darkness. Then glass started crashing and echoing through the cabin.

I aimed quickly and my two shots were immediately drowned out by a horrible, shrill scream. I gotten one of them.

"That's where the third bastard was. Sallie?...Sallie..."

I heard a moan next to me.

"You hit?"

"Can't talk." I heard him choke slightly.

"In the side, Tom. I think it's only a flesh wound."

In the darkness, I ripped his shirt away from his side. I could feel a slight gash, warm and sticky, as I took out my handkerchief to press down on the wound.

"It doesn't seem that bad. Put some pressure here and the bleeding should stop."

"I'll be okay...it just knocked the wind out of me."

"Sallie, can you move? We have to get the hell outta here."

"Just let me catch my breath. Just give me a minute."

"Now, look...when we open the door they're gonna make sure that all hell opens up on us...this is what we should do...we'll duck back and let 'em hit the open doorway, just long enough to locate their positions...then, I'm going to start firing...you make a dash for it...I'll be close behind you...I'm gonna get 'em...there's only two left."

I knew there was no sense in expecting anyone to call the cops...they would have been here by now...great neighborhood they picked...people too scared to get involved...taught to mind their own business...taught by who? Dave's kind?...Not when you hear all this racket.

"Sallie, if we stay here, it'll only be a matter of time..."

"Okay, Tom. I'm fine. Let's get going...hand me that guy's hardware. I can use an extra piece."

I crawled on my stomach to reach the man I had shot near the bed. As I was groping for his gun, I suddenly felt a searing pain in my shoulder. I've been shot. A slug tore into me and the bullet's impact practically spun me in a half circle. I heard two more shots ringing in my ears as the floor met my face.

"Tom?" I heard Sallie's voice, thankfully...Sallie was okay.

"Are you alright, Tom?"

My arm felt as if it was being torn away from my body. I winced, practically passing out.

"What happened? Guess they got a stray bullet in here."

"No, that bastard...by the table. He wasn't out cold, but he is now, permanently."

I glanced in the table's direction. He was lying there in a puddle of blood. I had been stupid again. I didn't finish him off before. Only Sallie's quick reflex had saved my life.

"Thanks, Sallie."

"Save your thanks until we get the fuck outta here. Can you make it?"

"Give me your belt to tighten around this wound or I'll lose too much blood."

This was great. Now the two of us were hit. Joan flashed through my mind. I had to get out...had to see her. I took a deep breath, fumbling with my arm, then rested for a minute.

"Sallie, when we go out the door, you turn left. Head towards the row of cabins and stay behind 'em. They should give us some protection until we reach my car. It's about two hundred yards away from here at the end of the row...the cabin marked, number ten...well, you'll recognize my car.

"And Sallie, if something happens...there's a letter in the glove compartment for Joan. Don't wait more than five minutes for me...then get going...OKAY?...let's go."

Sallie's hand was on my shoulder and he was silent.

"Tom, regardless of what happens, always remember, your friendship is priceless. I'm sorry I got you involved in this mess...I should've bought a house somewhere else...but if we do get out...I'm quitting the union...just like you wanted...maybe we both can just go somewhere and start over..."

"Let's go."

I opened the door and the moment I did, they started firing, bullets smacking the whole cabin.

"One is behind the car, Tom. You take that one."

"Yeah, I see him. The other is behind that tree on the left."

Sallie crouched down low waiting for his chance to spring out the door. The firing suddenly stopped. Sallie stood up and fired at the man behind the tree. I took on the one by the car as Sallie flew out the door running. He was halfway to the cabin when I saw a tiny burst from his gun. He was trying to give me some protection...

"Go, Sallie...go, Tom," I whispered to myself in the darkness.

I dashed through the open door firing at the car at the same time. We were gonna make it, I thought. I saw the man step out from behind the tree and aim a shot at Sallie. Sallie fired twice. The man raised his hands to his face and he sagged to the ground. Two down. One more bastard to go. I heard a bullet passing over my head. As I passed Sallie, I yelled.

"Keep going. We're almost there."

I reached the cabin first and threw myself to the ground. I turned around to give Sallie some cover, but only deadly quiet met me. I peered into the darkness. Sallie was lying on the ground where I had passed him. No, no. We're so close. I retraced my steps and hurled myself beside him...his heart was still beating. Thank God!

"Sallie? You got hit?"

He didn't answer...he was unconscious...there was no time to think. I would have to drag him. As I bent over to grab hold of him, a burning pain burst inside me so severe that it moved me backwards. I turned and saw Dave advancing towards me.

I fired instantly and got him. The bastard, son of a bitch had practically killed me. I wanted to continue slugging him...tear him to pieces. Maybe, I did. It all happened so quickly. But, Sallie was still lying there. He was still alive, but helpless. I was hit twice and bleeding again.

"Come on, Sallie, we're in the clear. We're safe. We got them both. Especially Dave. Wake up, Sallie. It's over. We can go home now."

Sallie did not wake up. I tried to stand up but I never made it. I fell back into the dirt and started soaking in my own blood. I had to get up again, but my chest was exploding and my head was spinning. I reached for Sallie's collar and pulled.

It seemed to take an eternity just to reach the car. I tried to lift Sallie into the car, but he slipped from my grasp and we both collapsed. I lost my wind again and lay there retching and hurting. Then I pulled myself up and shoved his body half way in. I had to crumple his legs to get him in the car. I staggered over to the driver's side, but I hit dirt again.

I don't know how long I was lying there. I could hardly reach the car door's handle. I finally gripped the door with both hands and managed to awkwardly stand.

"Help me, Sallie." There was no response. He didn't even move. He was still in the same slumped position. I tumbled into the driver's seat and partially fell on top of him. I reached over and felt for his heart. There was no heartbeat. He was dead.

"My friend...don't die. Please don't die," I practically screamed.

Maybe I was wrong. Yes, I had to be. It just seemed that he was dead because he was unconscious, and I was in so much pain. I started the car and moved it slowly down the path. In the background, sirens began to wail, and then lights began to flicker in the darkness, one by one like a Christmas tree lighting up.

"You bastard's. Too worried about your own hides to come out of your holes and lift a finger. It's all over now. Who needs you? Right, Sallie?" I shouted.

I drove out onto the highway. I thought, did I get rid of the guns? Funny thing to think when you're coughing up blood. I can't get caught. I've got to keep going. Sallie is going to make it. He's going to get out. Won't Joan be happy to see me. I have to get home...

The car began to move on its own. It almost seemed to rock me to sleep. I was so tired...so tired. This damn car was swerving all over the road but I couldn't control it. Better, though. I have to get home...Joan will take care of me...I just have to get there...God, my chest hurts so much...can't keep my eyes open anymore...Joan...sweet Joan...It's all dark...where are you?

CHAPTER 30

▼

THE RESCUE

Chapter Thirty

"Boy, what a mess! He crashed right into that wall. He must've been doing eighty..."

"Hey, lieutenant. Want me to bag the guns?" A man's voice bellowed in the distance.

My letter was somewhere. I had to think. In the glove compartment...in my jacket? All I heard were these men talking. Where was I? I couldn't remember. My chest hurt so much...I wanted to sleep so badly and could barely open my eyes. The smell of rubbing alcohol filled my nostrils as I saw two people dressed in white towering above me. I sensed a door was open somewhere because the air kept rushing in past me. I had to find Joan. And Sallie, my friend? Where are you? I kept dozing off, but still I kept hearing those men talking.

"The trooper said they'll probably die on the way to the hospital. They sure looked like they were dead before the car crashed. The one driving had two, three bullets in him...the other...one near the heart."

"That's nothing. You should see the mess down by the cabin."

"Sergeant, you can take it from here. See that this mess is cleaned up...and write it up."

Joan had miraculously arrived. A door slammed shut on me and the cool air stopped rushing in. Everything became silent and the men no longer talked. Then Sheila appeared, the two women staring blankly at each other with their pale, white faces breaking into sobbing. So that was it. We were dead already. They were visiting our bodies, weren't they? The stupid bastard's were making them ID us. But I could not quite see where we were. I watched Joan intently without being seen...as a ghost, I guess.

"Why, Tom? Why?...I feel so alone...this is just torture," Joan cried.

"I know," Sheila sobbed. "It's as if someone took my whole life from me...I didn't do anything to deserve this. Sallie was my whole life, for Christ sake."

"Tom, I keep telling myself I should have thrown myself at you and never let you leave that night...you came back...when you told Sheila about what Sallie really did for a living. I keep rehearsing it over and over again. I feel I'm almost going to go crazy...I still had a chance to change your mind...God...why did I let you go? I should've persuaded you somehow. This is all my fault...

"Maybe we can postpone this, Sheila. We can just call the funeral home and say the viewing will have to wait."

I lapsed into a daze...couldn't feel anything. I was all numb inside and kept blanking out as sirens screamed all around me. I tried so hard to get up. My Joan was still here and I wanted to hold her so much. This could not be, I could not be dead...then, a searing pain went through my whole body.

"I'm gonna need a doctor soon or I'm going to die...something," I groaned involuntarily. "Joan, is that you?"

"Oh God, he's hallucinating...can you hear me? Hang in there, talk to me. Tell me about Joan. We're almost at the hospital. Your buddy's still hanging in there too."

"I see her everywhere. My letter? Did she read my letter? Please, it's all there, Joan, JOAN!" I think I yelled.

"He's getting agitated. Better not encourage him to talk. He's lost so much blood...make him comfortable," someone inside the ambulance said.

"Joan, I see you everywhere I look. Please hold my hand."

I could feel something crash beneath me, like wheels hitting the pavement only I was above them and being pushed somehow, and sensed that people were moving very quickly around me. Faces and voices whizzed by me and the lights became very bright. The air felt warmer somehow. Hands grabbed me and I was hoisted onto some sort of flat surface.

"I need him out, now. Call the OR..." was all I remembered.

"Wait. I have to talk to him," yelled a man rushing to me waiving a badge at everyone, only he wasn't in a uniform.

"You, can't, and I don't care who you are. He's bleeding too badly. If you don't let us do our job you'll be talking to a corpse soon," the doctor said.

"Tom? Are you Tom Furcco?" the man continued ignoring their warnings, even as they started pushing him away.

"Are you Tom Furcco?"

"Yes," I mumbled. "Joan?"

"Joan is alright, Tom. We found your letter. Just tell me this quickly. If I can make a deal for you, will you take it?"

"Yeah"

CHAPTER 31

▼

THE DEAL

Chapter Thirty-One

"It was a stroke of good luck that the ambulance attendant heard you talk about that letter. This sure is a sweet deal, Tom."

"What I want to know, is where's my wife? I don't like that you haven't talked to her or even Sallie's wife yet? Why did you deliver and let her read that damn letter…what am I gonna do if she fuckin' commits suicide out of grief, you asshole? You promised us a visit with our wives. You gave me your word…before the testifying."

I shouted at the thin FBI man standing beside our beds. He was about sixty years old with dyed dark hair, dressed immaculately in a grey suit.

"Oh, calm down…for top bosses in the union you're acting like babies."

"Babies?…You think I'm testifying against the union after all these years because I'm a baby?"

Sallie tried to get up, but the gun shot wounds still hurt too much.

"Listen," the FBI agent continued. "I didn't stop by here today just to give you a get well card…your wives are alright…we've had 'em watched since you got here and no one has shown up…that's good…that means that your union friends really think you both are dead. I'm here to give you some good news."

"Good news? What fuckin' good news. We're both here wrapped up in bandages and morphine, hardly sleeping at all unless they give us a pill, always watching that God damn door waiting for one of John's crew…I tell you, John is gonna put a contract out on us…he'll find out we're still alive. We know too much."

"Listen, you leave everything to me," the FBI agent answered flatly.

"I'm tellin' you, I don't like it. Just yesterday, a new orderly was in here. He acted peculiar. How do you know he's not John Gervonte's plant or something?"

"Listen…are you gonna let me give you some good news or what? You have nothing to worry about. There's been an undercover detective, ever since you agreed to testify against the union. Everyone who walks in here belongs to me. This corner of the hospital is on the top floor. The public just thinks it's administration and offices, but it's really a very private sanitarium—for better paying patients. Not even the public can get to it unless you are cleared with a key to the locked elevator. So fuckin' relax.

"And, John Gervonte and his crew are going to go to jail for a very long time. Right now, warrants are being served for arson, assault, grand larceny, and antitrust crimes against fifty-two shops Both New York offices are completely surrounded and none of them are getting out. There are no leaks this time. The same thing is going on in Florida, New Orleans, Connecticut…it's a great day…what a round up…and, your wives are here, by the way."

"What?" both Tom and Sallie turned white and said the same word together.

"Joan? She knows?"

"Where's Sheila? You told her I'm still alive?"

"Well, not exactly. I told you we had to work this realistically. It's only tears for Christ sake, but it was very important for everyone to see them grieving and thinking you were dead. And we want everyone who sees them in this hospital to think so too. That's how we can protect you the most."

"Where's Sheila? She's so frail. I have to see her." Sallie tried to get up again.

"Not so fast…"

"The hell with the wounds!"

"I'm telling you, you asshole, that John's gonna find out we're still alive. Hell, he has so many connections, down to a few fucked up police. He's gonna find out…bet he even had our wives tailed here."

"No, we had them under surveillance since Joan received your letter.

"No. To everyone else, your wives are just here routinely. They have to identify your bodies in order for the hospital to release you for burying."

"Are you fuckin' stupid or something? Why are you doing this…putting my wife, our wives through so much?"

"Why didn't you just stage killing them too and float their bodies in a canal somewhere?"

"Don't your guys in Washington know what real grief is?"

"Sorry, fellas. But it had to be done this way. And, I told you, you're protected. Your own union crews are not going to find out that your still alive."

"You're so fuckin' sure? You know if I could, I wouldn't be talking to you at all. You really think you can make all four of us disappear? You don't know, John. He's no asshole. As soon as you arrest him, he'll figure, soon after that shooting involving Dave, Sallie and some guy called Romano? He'll ask around. He'll order a contract from even inside the pen. Now when am I gonna see my wife?"

"If you don't get me out of this bed, I'll kill somebody."

"Okay, okay. This is what I started to tell you. Your wives are down in the administrator's office. I'll get 'em sent up here for a visit? Just a short visit. It'll just look like they were taking them to ID your bodies"

"Can we get this over with already? I need to see my wife...my beautiful, Joan...you don't think when the two of 'em don't return home...it won't look suspicious? I'm telling you, I don't like this. He's gonna put a contract out."

The F.B.I. agent slipped out of the room and returned with Joan and Sheila.

Sheila passed out immediately. Joan tried to stand up but fell back in her seat.

"I can't believe it. God, God, thank you so much!" Joan practically knocked me out of bed rushing up to me. She had been clutching my letter in her hands and as she pushed it into mine, I could feel all her pain. It was completely covered with tears.

"Now get the tears over with and everything and everyone will feel better. Okay? A deal's a deal. I promised you a visit. Then we have to separate you again. You two will travel in a separate ambulance. We'll meet up with your wives at another location in a few days, and when you're well enough to testify, you will. Then, we'll transfer you and your wives one more time with new identities, just as I told you before."

"Can you get her some water or something?...Sheila, Sheila...don't get faint," Sallie cried out. "Yes, I'm really alive still."

"God, Joan, I love you so much."

Sheila began recovering, and both women started crying and we kept hugging each other over and over again.

"Ladies, please calm down," our agent said impatiently. "It's very important that you not talk about this. Your husbands' union have ears in a lot of places. You must make everyone around you believe your husbands are dead. All you are here for is to identify their bodies. And that's where you're going to pretend to do now. Only we are going to take you separately to an undisclosed location.

"Now, take a moment to compose yourselves, and let's go. Remember, you must look heart-broken still...I can only give you these few minutes. I know it's a shock, but you can talk later. I promise you ladies, you'll be seeing your husbands in a few days. It's for everyone's protection. It just has to be this way. Now, this way, quickly. And, NO talking."

Joan and Sheila were practically pushed out of the room by an agent.

"Let's give them a few minutes," our agent said. "Then we go too."

Sallie and I looked like two asshole's. There was so much to say and they were just gone. The agent glanced at his watch, and as usual, a few minutes turned into a silent eternity. When he finally opened the door, all we heard was gun fire.

CHAPTER 32

▼

TILL DEATH DO US PART

Chapter Thirty-Two

We were greeted with shouting, and men with guns running all over the place.

"Get them outta here!...Now!" someone shouted.

"Go, go..."

Hell, I wished I had a gun. I would've loved to have killed him. It was Vinnie. We were quickly pushed out the hallway and shoved to an exit as I saw his bloodied body on the floor. A gun was still in his hands.

"Get 'em in the elevator for Christ sake. Something went wrong. I dunno what yet."

"I told you, Sallie. They're not gonna give up. They're gonna find us where ever we go...damn. That fuckin' Vinnie. After all these years. What a son of a bitch. I'll kill 'em all yet."

"If I don't get to 'em first, Tom. I can't believe they got this close. They must've followed Joan and Sheila. Asshole Feds, can't arrange anything and keep it quiet...now, here we go again. I'm gonna personally kill that agent if he fuck's this up and we never see our wives again."

We were whisked to the basement out an exit to a waiting ambulance. We were barely tied down and secured, when the ambulance door slammed shut and we took off. We turned a corner, then halted. It was a back alley of some sort for deliveries. Gun fire was heard again. Someone ran up to the driver.

"Just get going! Don't waste any time!" he shouted.

I thought about Joan. Did she hear the guns go off? Did she know? What did she think of such a damn, two minute visit, and why should I even trust these guys now? Such, stupid, stupid asshole's...I could kill 'em. They really messed up and I was really, really getting pissed. At the same time, such sadness swelled up inside me, I found I could suddenly hardly talk. Was I really ever going to see her again? Why, God? We came so close to getting out of this, and now it was all lost again.

I had no idea if Sallie and I would be alive to see them again or how much time we had left. We were completely defenseless, recovering from painful, injuries without even any weapons. Talking to the driver was useless.

My letter? I still had it in my hand. She had read it and cried her heart out. Whatever was this all for? The union knew. What if it really happened? What if I had written my fate after all? She and Sheila were probably crying again as another vehicle rushed away with them. Did they somehow know that their husbands were this close to being dead?

I had tears in my eyes as Sallie looked away from me, strangely silent as well. I remembered when I had written that letter. It was when Sallie and Sheila first walked into my life again. Prophetic, wasn't it? Almost as if I always knew something bad was gonna come out of all of this? I read it again, trying to reach Joan in my thoughts, out there somewhere.

My Dearest Joan…Darling,

I love you…before I tell you anything else, I must tell you that.

This is the one letter I wrote that I hoped sincerely you would never read. But, if you are reading it, my next words are "I'm sorry."

I'm so sorry, honey, I blew it. I'm gone and all you have is the grief and heartache. If I could only come back and stop all this for you. Can I never have you in my arms again?

Fate, destiny has finally caught up with me. Call it what you want, it all adds up to the same ending.

You are everything to me. You gave me the most wonderful years of my life. I must have told you more than a thousand times that I love you. And now, I want to tell you this again…I love you, whole-heartedly and completely, with all my heart and all my soul.

Don't be sad. I loved my first wife and my very dear Connie a long time ago, but I never thought I would find such bliss again as I have with you. I have been blessed with unimaginable peace, contentment, and joy with you, that is beyond expressing in words.

I know what you are yelling at me now, darling. How could I have been so stupid as to jeopardize our happiness? Why aren't I home with you now? Why did I let someone else take all that was precious to both of us? I cannot ever give you a justifiable answer, Joan, my darling Joan. There are tears in my eyes as I write this.

If I could walk back from the grave, I would. I managed to run and hide for most of my life, and I was wrong to involve innocent people, like you. We always said when we began our new life together, that we had buried the past, but I know now, you can never really bury it. That's what spoiled everything.

Can you really leave behind your crimes? All those I am guilty of, all the terrible things I have done which I can never undo or pay for, and this was the biggest of them, to have loved you so, and so selfishly.

Please forgive me. Since the day I met you, I remembered how good and beautiful life can be. You showed me that. There isn't a day when I don't wonder how God could be so good to me, after all I've done. There's not a judge in the world who ever would have given me such a wonderful sentence, to meet you, to live with you, to hold you, to love you.

So, maybe this is inevitable. I was graced with a few years of brightness and happiness with you, my beautiful Joan, and now I have to pay for my past. I guess I converted to a new man too late. The past still ended up haunting me, my list of crimes, and now I must atone for my past sins. If it must be death, this is the best way.

But, don't feel sorry for me, Joan, and don't cry forever. Your face and presence will always be with me, yes, even beyond the grave, as they say. Don't cry your heart out over me. I was never good enough to deserve you. But somehow God, in his mercy, gave me this precious time with you. For this alone, I am thankful. It was more than I could have ever wished for or deserved.

I'm just sorry I had to drag you into this. We changed our names, we moved away to put that union mob behind us, but it was like building a bad house...I just tried to build one on quicksand, so sooner or later it was bound to fall. I dragged myself into a trap, and the further I went, the deeper the point of no return. I'm so sorry Joan...to have ever involved you in this...now, I have reached the end of the line and all you have are memories and pain.

Do not despair, Joan. I am sure you will love again, and I want that. I know there is little I can write to ease your heart and hurt right now, but do not become bitter.

Time heals all wounds, and it will heal yours too. You have been a perfect wife, and I know your love will save you. Maybe, you can go back to our home town. If you can, please find my boys and tell them I love them too. Explain to them why I left them behind. I didn't want them hurt. Maybe you can love them too and give them some solace. I would like that as a last dying wish.

Joan, our love for each other was so strong, it will not really ever die. It will always live somewhere deep inside my heart and within yours. Even though I am no longer with you to take care of you, don't be afraid. God will always watch over and protect you from all harm. That is the one thing I know...

I have left you everything. I know you will do right by the boys. There is enough money to take care of all of you for quite a while. There is an insurance policy, the deeds to the house and club, the bank books, and my will is in the locked desk drawer in the study.

You can sell the club and house as well. Maybe you should. It would be better for you to move somewhere else and start fresh. I was going to make Jake an offer, let him come in as a partner. Maybe you can give him one third of the proceeds when you sell. I'll leave that to you. I trust your judgment. I always have.

Leave the pain behind you, Joan, and know that you did something so special for a stupid, undeserving man, me. My love for you is, was, always unmeasurable. I was selfish...I just could not live without you.

Here is my one unselfish thought and wish for you...that someday you will once again find happiness and love. You have a full life ahead of you and your grief and loneliness will not last forever. This much I know. There is too much beauty inside of you, too much goodness, too much love.

I know you may say "never" now...that can never be. But remember, Joan, my dearest Joan, you're the kind that attracts love. You need a life with love and companionship. You need someone to share your joys and sorrows. I know you will find him again someday.

I love you. I love you so much.

Always yours, in love forever,
And may death never part us,
Tom

It was a three hours', very long drive. We were taken to a small, out of season hotel in the countryside, and miraculously arrived in one piece with no incidents. We sat in that cramped van so long their idea of a straight drive without stopping.

A housekeeper, I thought, greeted us at the back entrance, but I soon realized she worked for the FBI. They also carry us up the stairs, and got us in the room. At least they had plenty of painkillers.

They kept us together in one upstairs room that had two twin beds and a small eating area. It was pleasant enough for a short stay, but the view was dull and our days became monotonous. But it was better than jail. After awhile, the highlight everyday was when the linens were changed and the meals were served. The only bright thing was that our wives were expected to join us in a few days.

However, it was now the start of the fourth week and still they hadn't showed. Both Sallie and I were depressed. I mean, it had almost been a whole month now, and I couldn't take it much longer. It was windy that day and the leaves cluttered the view, but that's about all I had, that fucked up view hoping to see my wife in it soon. We were out in the middle of nowhere. I could only see the last ten feet or so of the driveway that led to the back, not the main entrance or main road itself or any traffic. And, no one drove up this back driveway.

It was disgusting, like climbing the walls. Nothing to do, nothing to see, and no information. They kept our room's windows and door locked, and we were not permitted to move freely throughout the building. They wouldn't even let us read a newspaper, and NO phone.

Just like two trapped animals in a cage, that's what we were. They might as well have put us in the pen, except the decor and food were better here. No one would answer our questions about where our wives were.

I suddenly felt very old. Sallie and I had said little to each other for the past few hours. We just kept staring out that damn window in silence.

"What could have happened? I just don't get it." Sallie said suddenly, motioning to the empty countryside.

"How long do they think they're gonna keep us here, and where the hell are our wives? Why, God, why?" There were tears in Sallie's eyes, and this was a man who did not cry.

"They were followed, Sallie. I can just feel it. I'm gonna kill that motherfucker if anything has happened to 'em."

"And they won't tell us anything. You think I'm gonna testify if my wife is kidnaped or dead?"

"And that bastard—the one who just sits in the hallway outside our room—still he says nothing. We're prisoners practically. Fuck."

"Should I pick the lock on the door?"

"How far would we fuckin' get? The bastard's always there and it's a little hard to take him in the shape we're in."

"I don't know. Maybe we could get down the stairs alright."

"How many others do you think we might run into?"

"What difference does any of this make now? Something has gone wrong, very wrong. Couldn't even spend more than two damn minutes with her."

"I keep wishing that maybe a car will pull up, and I will see Joan again, smiling, laughing, happy...why are they keeping us here and not telling us something?"

"I think I hear our FBI warden in the hallway."

"Better lower our voices. He's gonna ask us if we need something."

"Maybe he wants to bring up our testifying again?"

"He doesn't get it, does he? No wives, no deal."

"Oh, I think he fuckin' got it. I won't talk. No wives, no deal."

"I still say we should jump him. Just run."

"Yeah, but the problem is they're the only ones who know where Joan and Sheila are, whether alive or dead. Either way they got us by the balls. Huh?"

"I just can't believe how fucked up this whole thing has gotten. I'm not gonna testify, I tell you."

"You think they used our wives to give out a false trail?"

"I'll kill 'em all if they put her in danger."

"Is that why no newspapers to read? So we can't find out if they were hurt or in an accident?"

The door opened very quietly while we were still talking. Neither of us noticed at first.

"You guys want some coffee or something?" The FBI warden suddenly said.

"I love you so much." Joan barely found her voice, tears running down her face.

"Sal…darling", Sheila said softly at the same time.

Both Sallie and I turned around as the man from the hallway ushered in our two wives, smiled, and closed the door.

978-0-595-82633-9
0-595-82633-4

Printed in the United States
96402LV00004B/385-408/A